Published by Sophene 2019

Georgian Tales was first published in 2019 by Sophene Pty Ltd.

These tales were originally translated to the English language by
John Oliver and Marjory Wardrop.

www.sophenebooks.com

ISBN-13: 978-1-925937-11-4

GEORGIAN TALES

A COLLECTION OF CLASSIC GEORGIAN FOLK TALES

GEORGIAN TALES

A COLLECTION OF CLASSIC GEORGIAN FOLK TALES

CONTENTS

THE MAN AND THE BEAR

A man and a bear became friends. The man invited the bear to his house, and made a feat for him; when the bear took his leave and went away, the man kissed him, and made his wife do the same. She perceived the unpleasant odor of the bear, and said: "I am not fond of guests with stinking mouths." The bear then departed. Afterwards the man went out to the forest, and took an axe with him to cut firewood. The bear went, and greeted the man, then said "Strike me on the head and wound me." The man refused, but the bear insisted, so he struck him with the axe and broke his head. The bear went away into the woods, and the man went home. When they met, about a month later, the bear said to him "The wound you gave me with the axe is healed, but my heart, wounded by your wife's tongue, is still sore."

THE KING'S COUNSEL TO HIS THIRTY SONS

There was once a famous king who had thirty sons. When the time of his death came near, he had thirty arrows brought, bound them together, and then tried to break them, but could not; then he took them one by one and broke them all, saying to his children: "If you stay together, the foe cannot destroy you, as I was unable just now to break the arrows bound together; but if you separate, the enemy will ruin you and your kin one by one. If unity and love be among you, you shall overcome the enemy and rule unshaken; if you are disobedient one to another, your destruction is inevitable."

THE MAN THAT BURIED GOLD IN THE EARTH

A certain man buried much gold in the earth. Every day he went and looked at the spot. Another man said: "I will go and dig in the place he looks at so often and see what he has there." He cane by night, dug up the gold, and took it away, leaving a big stone instead. When the owner went to see his gold, he found the big stone. He began to weep and grieve bitterly. The thief came up to him and asked: "Why do you weep?" He replied: "I buried my gold, not wishing to spedn it, and now somebody has stolen it, and left a big stone in its place." The man who had dug up the gold said: "Woe! Why do you weep? If you did not wish to spend the gold, is it not all the same to you whether gold or stone lies there in the ground?"

THE THREE SISTERS AND THEIR STEPMOTHER

Once upon a time there was a peasant who had three daughters. This man's wife was dead, so he took to himself another. The stepmother hated the girls like the plague. Every day she bothered her husband, saying: 'Take away these daughters of yours, and get rid of them.' Sometimes she yielded to their father's requests, sometimes she gave way to her dislike. At last she could bear it no longer: she became ill, went to bed, took with her crisp, flat bread, and began to moan. She turned on one side, made the loaves crack, and cried out: 'My sides are breaking. Oh! Turn me on my other side!' The cause of all this was her stepdaughters, so her husband, seeing that nothing was to be done, consented to get rid of them.

He went away into the forest. There he saw a large apple-tree bearing fruit; underneath it he dug a deep hole, took an apple for each, and went home. When he came in, he gave each her apple. The girls liked the taste of the apples, and said to their father: 'Where did you find these? Can you not bring some more?' The father replied: 'There are many of these apples in the forest, but I have not time to bring more. If you like, you can come with me; I will shake them down, you can gather them up and bring them away.' The girls were delighted, and went with their father.

Their father had secretly covered up the hole, and said to the girls: 'Here are the apples. I will shake them down, but until I tell you do not gather them up. Then, when I speak, you can all scramble for them, and whoever picks up an apple, it is hers.' The father went up to the tree, and when he had shaken it well, called out to his daughters: 'Now, catch who can!' The girls suddenly rushed on to the covering, which could not bear their weight; it fell into the hole, taking with it the three girls. Their father threw them in a great many apples, left them, and went away.

The girls could not at first understand their father's conduct, but then they saw that he had brought them into the wood on purpose, and said: 'Our wicked stepmother is to blame for this!' but there was no help for it, so these three little maidens sat down and wept. They wept and wept until their faces were pale; their tears shook heaven above and the earth beneath. At last the apples were finished. They thought and thought, and decided that each should let blood from her little finger, and that they should eat her whose blood tasted sweetest. They let blood, and it was agreed by all that the youngest sister's was sweetest. She said: 'O sisters! Do not eat me. I have three apples hidden; eat them, and perhaps God will help us.'

Then she bent on her knees, and prayed to God: 'O God, for your name's sake, I beg you, let one of my hands turn into a pickaxe, and the other into a shovel.' God heard her prayer. One of her hands changed into a pickaxe, and the other into a shovel. With one hand she dug a hole, and with the other shovelled away the earth. She dug and dug until she came to a mouse's hole. She took those nuts, little nuts, and gave them to her sisters. She went on digging, and broke down a stable wall. This stable belonged to the king, and almonds and raisins were strewed about in it. The girls used to go to the stable; they stole the almonds and raisins, and ate them. The grooms were astonished, and said: 'Who can it be that steals the almonds and raisins? The horses are dying of starvation.'

The little maiden, in her digging, next broke the window

of an old woman's hut. Every morning the mistress of this hut went to mass. Feeling sorry for the old woman, the girls stole into the hut, cleaned and tidied everything, put beans on the fire to cook, broke off sufficient bread for themselves, and stole away again. When the old woman came home she was filled with surprise. Who could have been there and stolen her bread? Perhaps she could find out. She did not go to mass next day. She rolled herself in a mat, and stuck herself up, like a stick, near the door. The girls came; they thought the old woman had gone to mass, and stole into the hut one by one. The old woman watched from the mat with both her eyes, and she could scarcely believe what she saw. She saw the three maidens enter--each more beautiful than the other, all fair, as if the sun had never frowned upon them. She gazed and gazed until she could bear it no longer: she threw off the mat, seized one of them in her arms, and said: 'Who are you, that you are so angelic? Are you human or an angel?' The maiden replied: 'We are three sisters, we are human. Thus and thus has it befallen us.' And she told their tale to the old woman, who was delighted that she had found the three sisters. She guarded them as the light of her eyes, and, when she went out, turned up baskets over them, that none should see them and take them away.

Once the woman went to mass. She left the girls under baskets, and shut the doors. Then the idea came into the girls' heads that they would like some raisins. They rose, took off the baskets, and crept into the stable. Just as they were beginning to steal raisins, the groom hastened in, seized the three sisters, and took them before the king. The king asked them who they were, and they told him all their history. The king said: 'Tell me, what can you do?' The eldest sister said: 'I can weave such a carpet that every man in you army could sit on it, and still half of it would not be unrolled.' The second sister said: 'I can cook enough food in an egg-shell to feed yours army, and when they have eaten, half yet shall remain.' The king said to the youngest: 'What can you do?' She replied: 'I can bear golden-haired boys.' The king was pleased with this answer, and wedded her. He tried her sisters' skill, but the eldest could not weave a carpet large enough for one man, while the food cooked by the second sister would not have satisfied a bird. The king became angry, and said to his wife: 'If you deceive me too, none of you shall live.'

Some time passed, and the youngest sister was with child. At that time the king's enemy came against him, and he prepared to go forth to battle. Before he set out he left this message: 'If my wife bears a son, let a sword be suspended over the door; if she bears a daughter, let a spinning-wheel be hung up.' Shortly after this his wife went to bed. Her sisters would allow no one to enter the bedroom; they tended her and nursed her themselves.

The king's wife brought forth a golden-haired boy. Her two sisters were angry that their youngest sister should be proved truthful in the sight of the king, while they were liars; they wished her also to appear untruthful. They arose, and, without the mother's knowledge, took away the golden-haired boy, and put in his place a puppy dog. They did not dare to kill the child, so they made a box, laid him in it, and put it in a river. The river carried it away, and it stuck in a millrace. The race was dammed up and the mill stopped. The miller came out, and saw the box fixed in the race; he took it up and opened it. Behold, there lay a golden-haired child! He was childless, so he took it home and brought it up. In the meantime the sisters hung up a pestle over the door. The king returned from the battle and saw the pestle. He was very much surprised, and said: 'What does this mean? What has my wife brought forth?' They said: 'A puppy.' The king was very angry, but thought: 'Perhaps some one has done this; I will wait and see if she has a son.'

A year passed, and his wife was again with child. One day, when the king was out hunting, a golden-haired boy was born. The sisters, as before, would allow no one in the room. They took the child away secretly, and put a kitten in its place. They again put the child in a box in the river, and the miller found it again. The sisters hung the pestle over the door. When the king returned from the chase, and saw the pestle, he burned with fires of rage, and sparks shot from his eyes. He took his wife out, caused her to be wrapped in a bull's skin, and bound to a column in front of the palace. Every one who passed by was ordered to spit in her face and strike her. Thus unjustly did he torture an innocent being! The miller loved the two golden-haired children as if they were the apple of his eye. They became very wise, brave, and handsome, and grew as much in a day as other children grow in a year.

Once when the king was out hunting, he saw a group of children playing, but among them were two who far excelled the others. The king was very much taken with these two children, and could not withdraw his eyes from them. He looked and looked, and would never have been tired of looking; he wished to gaze on them forever. He noticed how strongly they resembled himself. He was astonished, and said to himself: 'Who can these children be, who are so like myself?' But he could not guess the truth. Just then, while playing, the cap fell from the head of one of the brothers, and showed his golden hair. The king was struck, and inquired: 'Whose children are these?' He was told they were the miller's sons.

The next day the king gave a banquet, and invited the miller and his golden-haired sons. When the children came into the king's courtyard, they saw a woman bound to a column, and they looked long, and knew that this must be their mother. The cook was roasting a pheasant. The elder brother went inside, took the spit from the cook, sat down by the fireside, and turned the pheasant round. When it became red and was cooked, he began to tell a tale. All ears were pricked up, and the people looked into his face. The boy began to tell his mother's tale. After he had told how his mother bore the golden-haired boys, and how the sisters were so treacherous, he concluded by saying: 'If this story is true, the bull's skin will burst, and my mother be free.' And the bull's skin burst, and his mother came in.

When the story was quite finished, his younger brother came in and took the spit in his hand, and said: 'If all my brother's tale is true and this is indeed our mother, this roast pheasant will have feathers and fly away.' Feathers appeared on the roast pheasant, and it flew off. The people gazed open-mouthed. The astonished king commanded the jealous sisters to be brought, bound them to horses' tails, and had them dragged about. The king took his wife and children into the palace, and rejoiced greatly that he had learnt the truth and found his golden-haired sons.

THE GOOD-FOR-NOTHING

There was once a good-for-nothing man, who had a nasty wife. This wife would give him no rest. She harassed him, saying: 'You must go away, go travel and search for something; you see how poor we are.' At last the husband could no longer bear her reproaches, so he arose and went.

He went forth, he himself knew not where he was going.

He travelled on, and when he had ascended the ninth mountain from where he started, he saw a large house, and in this house devis[1] dwelt. He came near and saw in the middle of the room a fire, round which the devis were sitting, warming their hands. He went in and spoke in a friendly manner to them, and sat down by the fire. The devis treated him well, for he had spoken them fair. He stayed with them by day and by night; he ate with them, he drank with them, he slept with them; he was like their youngest brother.

These devis possessed a wishing-stone. When they were assembled together, they took out the stone: if they wished for dinner, dinner appeared; if they wanted supper, they wished for supper, and lo! What they wished for heartily appeared before their eyes. They lived thus without care, they had no kind of sorrow, and this was just what our good-for-nothing liked; he approved of this life, and wanted to steal the wishing-stone.

Once when the devis were in a deep sleep, the good-for-nothing silently slipped out of the bedroom, took the wishing-stone, and came to the door. He wished the door to open, and sure enough it began to creak. It creaked and called out:

---

1 Devis, in Georgian mythology, are multi-headed ogres whose heads regenerate any time they are cut off (like the Greek hydra).

'The guest has stolen the wishing-stone.' The good-for-nothing turned back, put the stone in its place, went into the bedroom, and pretended to be asleep. The creaking of the door awoke the devis; they jumped up and looked; they found the wishing-stone in its place, and the good-for-nothing in a sweet slumber. They rejoiced, closed the door, and went to sleep again. When they had fallen into a profound sleep, the good-for-nothing rose up, took the stone, came to the door, and, when he wished it to open, it began to creak out: 'The guest has stolen the wishing-stone.' The good-for-nothing turned back, again put the wishing-stone in its place, went into the bedroom and began to snore as if he were asleep. The devis awoke and looked, but the stone was in its place, and the good-for-nothing snoring. They were surprised, but shut the door, and went to sleep.

The good-for-nothing did this trick over and over again. The devis were angry, and furiously jumped up, pulled down the door, and put it in the fire. When the door was burned, and the devis slept again, the good-for-nothing rose up, put the wishing-stone in his pocket, and left the house. The next morning, when the devis awoke, they saw that neither the good-for-nothing nor the wishing-stone was there any longer. They looked everywhere and could not find it. The good-for-nothing went on his way joyfully; he no longer had any care or thought; he rejoiced that now he could live without trouble. He went on, and met on the road a man with a big stick. This man said: 'Brother, give me something to eat.' The good-for-nothing put his hand in his pocket, and took out the wishing-stone. He wished, and there appeared before them everything ready for eating. When they had finished their meal, the man with the stick said: 'Come, I will exchange my stick with you for this stone.' 'What is the use of you stick?' inquired the good-for-nothing. 'If any one stretches out his hand and calls, "Out, stick!" the stick will fall upon the person in front of its master.' The good-for-nothing made the exchange, and went away a short distance; then he said, 'Out, stick!' and stretched it out towards its former master. It struck him until all his bones were made soft. When he had been well beaten, the good-for-nothing came, took his stone, and went on his way with the stick.

He went on and saw a man with a sword, who said: 'Brother, give me something to eat.' The good-for-nothing took out his wishing-stone, and immediately meat and drink appeared before them. When he had eaten sufficiently, the man said: 'Come, I will give you this sword in exchange for the stone.' 'What is the use of you sword?' inquired the good-for-nothing. 'Whoever possesses it can, if he choose, cut off a hundred thousand heads.'

He exchanged his wishing-stone for the sword, and went away. After waiting a short time, he said, 'Out, stick!' and pointed to the former owner of the sword. The stick approached and beat the man mercilessly. Then the good-for-nothing took the wishing-stone and went away.

He went on again until he met a man with a piece of felt, who said: 'Brother, give me something to eat.' The good-for-nothing man took out his wishing-stone, wished, and immediately a delicious repast appeared. When he had eaten all he wanted, the man said: 'Come, I will give you my cloth in exchange for this stone.' 'What is the use of you cloth?' inquired the good-for-nothing. 'If a man's head is cut off, one only has to take a piece of this cloth and apply it; his head will stick on again, and he will live.' The good-for-nothing gave him the stone, took the cloth, and went away. When he had gone a little way, he said, 'Out, stick!' and the stick beat the man till he was like a wrinkled quince. The good-for-nothing took his stone and travelled on.

At last he came to his home. He placed the stick behind the door, greeted his wife and spoke thus: 'Wife, see what I have brought,' and he showed her the sword, cloth, and wishing-stone. His wife looked on him with contempt, opened her mouth, and cast all the dirt in the world on his head. The good-for-nothing bore it till he could bear it no longer, so he called, 'Out, stick!' The stick beat her woefully. Then he made his little children sit down, took out his wishing-stone, wished the table to be laid, where the rarest delicacies were placed. They enjoyed their dinner, while the beaten wife silently looked down and sulked. She bore it for a time, but at last she could bear it no longer, and came and embraced her husband's knees. Her husband forgave her, and they caressed one another lovingly.

After some time, this wishing-stone made him quite rich, so that all their dishes were made of gold. Once the wife said to her husband: 'You must invite the king and give him a great banquet.' Her husband said: 'Do you not know, the king is an envious man; when he sees these things, he will take them from us, and put us in prison.' His wife pleaded and whined until her husband consented.

They invited the king, and made ready a magnificent banquet. When the feast was finished, the king demanded the wishing-stone. The good-for-nothing said he could not spare it. The king was enraged, and sent his whole army to take it away by force. 'This will not do at all,' said the good-for-nothing to himself; 'since they are going to try and force me, I shall show my strength.' While he spoke, he pointed the sword at the army, and the stick at the king. The heads of all the army were cut off, and the stick beat the envious king.

The king begged and prayed for mercy: 'Only bring my soldiers back to life again, and I swear I will leave you in peace.' Then the good-for-nothing arose, took the felt and laid a piece on the neck of each soldier, and the army was restored to life. The king no longer dared to show his hostility, the good-for-nothing's wife obeyed him in everything, and they lived happily ever afterwards.

THE FROG'S SKIN

There were once three brothers who wished to marry. They said: 'Let us each shoot an arrow, and each shall take his wife from the place where the arrow falls.' They shot their arrows; those of the two elder brothers fell on noblemen's houses, while the youngest brother's arrow fell in a lake. The two elder brothers led home their noble wives, and the youngest went to the shore of the lake. He saw a frog creep out of the lake and sit down upon a stone. He took it up and carried it back to the house. All the brothers came home with what fate had given them; the elder brothers with the noble maidens, and the youngest with a frog.

The brothers went out to work, the wives prepared the dinner, and attended to all their household duties; the frog sat by the fire croaking, and its eyes glittered. Thus they lived together a long time in love and harmony.

At last the sisters-in-law wearied of the sight of the frog; when they swept the house, they threw out the frog with the dust. If the youngest brother found it, he took it up in his hand; if not, the frog would leap back to its place by the fire and begin to croak. The noble sisters did not like this, and said to their husbands: 'Drive this frog out, and get a real wife for your brother.' Every day the brothers bothered the youngest. He replied, saying: 'This frog is certainly my fate, I am woryou of no better, I must be faithful to it.' His sisters-in-law persisted in telling their husbands that the brother and his frog must be sent away, and at last they agreed.

The young brother was now left quite desolate: there was no one to make his food, no one to stand watching at the door. For a short time a neighboring woman came to wait upon him, but she had no time, so he was left alone. The man became very melancholy.

Once when he was thinking sadly of his loneliness, he went to work. When he had finished his day's labor, he went home. He looked into his house and was struck with amazement. The sideboard was well replenished; in one place was spread a cloth, and on the cloth were many different kinds of tempting viands. He looked and saw the frog in its place croaking. He said to himself that his sisters-in-law must have done this for him, and went to his work again. He was out all day working, and when he came home he always found everything prepared for him.

Once he said to himself: 'I will see for once who is this unseen benefactor, who comes to do good to me and look after me.' That day he stayed at home; he seated himself on the roof of the house and watched. In a short time the frog leaped out of the fireplace, jumped over to the doors, and all round the room; seeing no one there, it went back and took off the frog's skin, put it near the fire, and came forth a beautiful maiden, fair as the sun; so lovely was she that man could not imagine anything prettier. In the twinkling of an eye she had tidied everything, prepared the food and cooked it. When everything was ready, she went to the fire, put on the skin again, and began to croak. When the man saw this he was very much astonished; he rejoiced exceedingly that God had granted him such happiness. He descended from the roof, went in, caressed his frog tenderly, and then sat down to his tasty supper.

The next day the man hid himself in the place where he had been the day before. The frog, having satisfied itself that nobody was there, stripped off its skin and began its good work. This time the man stole silently into the house, seized the frog's skin in his hand and threw it into the fire. When the maiden saw this she entreated him, she wept—she said: 'Do not burn it, or you shalt surely be destroyed'—but the man had burnt it in a moment. 'Now, if you happiness be turned to misery, it is not my fault,' said the sorrow-stricken woman.

In a very short time the whole countryside knew that the man who had a frog now possessed in its place a lovely woman, who had come to him from heaven.

The lord of the country heard of this, and wished to take her from him. He called the beautiful woman's husband to him and said: 'Plant a barn of wheat in a day, or give me your wife.' When he had spoken thus, the man was obliged to consent, and he went home melancholy.

When he went in he told his wife what had taken place. She reproached him, saying: 'I told you what would happen if you burn the skin, and you did not heed me; but I will not blame you. Don't be sad; go in the morning to the edge of the lake from which I came, and call out: "Mother and Father! I pray you, lend me your swift bulls"—lead them away with you, and the bulls will in one day plough the fields and plant the grain.' The husband did this.

He went to the edge of the lake and called out: 'Mother and Father! I entreat you, lend me your swift bulls today.' There came forth from the lake such a team of oxen as was never seen on sea or land.

The youth drove the bulls away, came to his lord's fields, and ploughed and sowed them in one day.

His lord was very much surprised. He did not know if there was anything impossible to this man, whose wife he wanted. He called him a second time, and said: 'Go and gather up the wheat you hast sown, that not a grain may be wanting, and that the barn may be full. If you dost not this, you wife is mine.'

'This is impossible,' said the man to himself. He went home to his wife, who again reproached him, and then said: 'Go to the lake's edge and ask for the jackdaws.'

The husband went to the edge of the lake and called out: 'Mother and Father! I beg you to lend me your jackdaws to-day.' From the lake came forth flocks of jackdaws; they flew to the ploughed ground, each gathered up a seed and put it into the barn.

The lord came and cried out: 'There is one seed short; I know each one, and one is missing.' At that moment a jackdaw's caw was heard; it came with the missing seed, but owing to a lame foot it was a little late.

The lord was very angry that even the impossible was possible to this man, and could not think what to give him to do.

He puzzled his brain until he thought of the following plan. He called the man and said to him: 'My mother, who died in this village, took with her a ring. If you go to the other world and bring that ring here to me, it is well; if not, I shall take away you wife.'

The man said to himself: 'This is quite impossible.' He went home and complained to his wife. She reproached him, and then said: 'Go to the lake and ask for the ram.'

The husband went to the lake and called out: 'Mother and Father! give me your ram today, I pray you.' From the lake there came forth a ram with twisted horns; from its mouth issued a flame of fire. It said to the man: 'Mount on my back!'

The man sat down, and, quick as lightning, the ram descended towards the lower regions. It went on and shot like an arrow through the earth.

They travelled on, and saw in one place a man and woman sitting on a bull's skin, which was not big enough for them, and they were like to fall off. The man called out to them: 'What can be the meaning of this, that this bull skin is not big enough for two people?' They said: 'We have seen many pass by like you, but none has returned. When you come back we shall answer you question.'

They went on their way and saw a man and woman sitting on an axe-handle, and they were not afraid of falling. The man called out to them: 'Are you not afraid of falling from the handle of an axe?' They said to him: 'We have seen many pass by like you, but none has returned. When you come back we shall answer your question.'

They went on their way again, until they came to a place where they saw a priest feeding cattle. This priest had such a long beard that it spread over the ground, and the cattle, instead of eating grass, fed on the priest's beard, and he could not prevent it. The man called out: 'Priest, what is the meaning of this? Why is you beard pasture for these cattle?' The priest replied: 'I have seen many pass by like you, but none has returned. When you come back I shall answer your question.'

They journeyed on again until they came to a place where they saw nothing but boiling pitch, and a flame came forth from it--and this was hell. The ram said: 'Sit firmly on my back, for we must pass through this fire.' The man held fast, the ram gave a leap, and they escaped through the fire unhurt.

There they saw a melancholy woman seated on a golden throne. She said: 'What is it, my child? what troubles you? what has brought you here?' He told her everything that had happened to him. She said: 'I must punish this very wicked child of mine, and you must take him a casket from me.' She gave him a casket, and said: 'Whatever you do, do not open this casket yourself, take it with you, give it to you lord, and run quickly away from him.'

The man took the casket and went away. He came to the place where the priest was feeding the cattle. The priest said: 'I promised you an answer; hearken unto my words. In life I loved nothing but myself, I cared for nothing else. My flocks I fed on other pastures than my own, and the neighbouring cattle died of starvation; now I am paying the penalty.'

Then he went on to the place where the man and woman were sitting on the handle of the axe. They said: 'We promised you an answer; hearken unto our words. We loved each other too well on earth, and it is the same with us here.'

Then he came to the two seated on the bull skin, which was not big enough for them. They said: 'We promised you an answer; hearken unto our words. We despised each other in life, and we equally despise each other here.'

At last the man came up on earth, descended from the ram, and went to his lord. He gave him the casket and quickly ran away. The lord opened the casket, and there came forth fire, which swallowed him up. Our brother was thus victorious over his enemy, and no one took his wife from him. They lived lovingly together, and blessed God as their deliverer.

FATE

There was once a mighty king, who had an only son. When this son grew up every princess was in love with him. The king was very desirous that his son should be early settled in life. He chose for him a princess, whom he proposed he should marry. The son objected very much, saying: 'It is not my fate to be united to this maiden; I shall not marry her.'

Some time after this the youth came to his father and said: 'I entreat you, let me go forth and seek my fortune, and give me three bags of money.' The king granted his request. The prince prepared everything, and set out on his journey.

He travelled on until he met a stranger; this stranger was an angel, clad in the form of a man. He inquired of the prince: 'Where art you going? what seekest thou?' The prince told him all, and that he wished to learn what was written in the book of fate for him. Then this stranger showed him a beautiful palace, and said: 'There you wilt learn you fate.'

The prince thanked him, and set out for the palace. When he arrived in the courtyard, he looked round, and saw notes lying about. He began to examine them, but, for a long time, he searched in vain. Then there came from the palace another man, who said to the prince: 'What dost you want, brother? what seekest thou?' The prince answered: 'I am seeking for the letter in which my fate is written.' 'Why seekest you there? those are only poor folks' fates, kings' fortunes are written inside. Come with me and I shall show you yours,' said the unknown.

The prince entered the house. The unknown searched for his fate, and called him. Inside was written: 'Such-and-such a prince will marry a weaver's daughter who has been ill for nine years.' He read this out, and the prince was struck with horror. 'I shall change my fate,' said the prince to himself. He took his letter of fate, and went to seek the weaver's daughter.

He went on and on, and was in a thick forest when the shades of evening fell. He wandered on in the hope of finding shelter, and at last he saw the glimmer of a light. He came to a hut, and asked permission to remain there during the night. The master of the house replied: 'Son, you art a great man, we have nothing befitting you rank, but we can give you the best we have, for a guest is a gift of God.' The prince stayed there that night, and his host grudged him nothing. When they had finished supper, the prince noticed that somebody was having a meal in another room. He said to his host: 'I hope that you wilt not think me inquisitive if I ask who is in the other room, and what is the meaning of this?' Then the host told him the following tale:

'I am a weaver, and from day to day can barely live. God has given me nobody to help me in my work. I have an only daughter, and she is an invalid. For nine years she has not risen from her bed; I can assure you she gives me no help.' When the prince heard this, he bit his little finger with vexation, and became melancholy. He did not close his eyes that night. He was thinking all the time how he might get rid of his fate.

In the middle of the night, when every one was snoring and slept like the dead, the prince rose silently, stole from his bedchamber, and quietly entered the room of the weaver's daughter. When he saw her he was inwardly troubled, he drew forth his dagger, and plunged it into her. Then he noiselessly went away, left his money behind him, and stole forth into the night.

He went home to his father, and complained of the evil

fate written for him. His father was very indignant at this, but hid his anger, and comforted his son.

Some time passed. One day the prince went out to hunt. He saw in a lonely wood a beautiful palace, and, in the palace, a maiden fair as the sun. The prince could have gazed for ever on her beauty. He looked a long time, then looking from a distance would not satisfy him. He spurred his horse, and when he came near he was even more struck with the loveliness of the maiden. He descended from his horse, came to her and asked her to marry him. When he had heard with joy her sweet words of consent, he went gaily home.

On the way, his head swam with pleasure at the thought of the welcome change; instead of the unhappy fate promised him, he was to have such a beautiful wife. He told his father what had happened to him, and asked him to prepare for the wedding. The king rejoiced at the happiness of his beloved son, and made preparations for a grand wedding.

Some days after they were married, the prince laid his hand on his lovely wife's heart, and felt something hard like a wart. He said: 'What is this?' His wife replied: 'I am a poor weaver's daughter; for nine years I lay in bed, a helpless invalid, yellow as a cucumber. Once there came a youth to my father's house for shelter. He plunged his dagger into me, then fled with haste, and went on his way. I was very sick, but my mother put a plaster on my side and I was completely cured. The guest left three bags of money behind him, and with these we bought a beautiful palace, my father gave up weaving, and we lived without a care.' When the prince heard this, he said: 'O God! You decrees are not vain and futile!' Then he told his beloved wife all that had happened to him.

GHVTHISAVARI

(I AM OF GOD)

There was once a king, who had a daughter so beautiful, that he was in constant fear lest some one should carry her away by force and marry her. So he had a huge tower built in the sea. He shut his daughter up in this tower, with an attendant, and felt relieved.

Some time passed, when one day the attendant noticed something floating on the water. She was surprised when she saw that it was a large apple. She stretched out her dress, and the sea waves rolled in and left the apple in her skirt; she took it in her hand, and ran to her mistress. The beautiful maiden had never in her life seen such a big apple, and was very much astonished. After dinner she peeled it, gave the skin to her companion, who quickly finished it, and ate the inside herself.

In a short time they both became pregnant. The king was informed of this. On hearing the news, he pressed his head between his hands, and could not contain his wrath. He commanded one of his huntsmen, saying: 'Go to the tower in the sea, take thence my daughter and her companion, and carry them to the wildest and most desert spot in my kingdom. Kill them, and bring me their hearts and livers to show me that they are dead. No one must know this story, save you and me; if it becomes known it shall cost you you life.'

The huntsman went to the tower, and declared the king's orders to the princess and her companion. The beautiful maiden said: 'What will it avail you to kill us? Take us to a lonely place, and no one will know whether we are dead or alive.'

The huntsman was not moved by these entreaties; he

took them to a desert place, drew his dagger and was about to strike the fatal blow, but at the last moment he felt sorry for them, and gave up his intention. He caught two hares, killed them instead of the women, took out their hearts and livers, and returned with them to the king. The king believed them to be the hearts and livers of the princess and her attendant; he gave the huntsman gifts, and sent him away.

The princess and her companion were left alone in the wild wood, and they had nothing to eat and drink.

In a short time the princess brought forth a beautiful boy, and the attendant, eight tiny little dogs. The princess called her son Ghvthisavari (I am of God). He grew as much in a day as other children grow in a year; he became so handsome, brave, and strong, that everybody loved him.

Ghvthisavari used to go out hunting; he took his dogs with him, and provided game for his mother and her companion.

Once he went into a town to a smith, and asked him to make a bow and arrows. The smith made from nine litras of iron (a litra = 9 lbs.) a bow and arrows. Ghvthisavari bent it. Then the smith added more iron, and made the bow again. Ghvthisavari slung his arrows over his shoulders, his dogs followed him, and he went away. On the way he hunted, and took food home to his mother.

The next day he went to hunt again. He shot an arrow and killed a goat, he shot another, and killed a stag; he drew his bow a third time, and his arrow stuck in a devis' house. In this house there were five brothers, devis--one two-headed, one three-headed, one five-headed, one nine-headed, and one ten-headed--and their mother, who had only one head. They saw an arrow suddenly fall down and stick in the fire. They all jumped up and pulled the arrow to draw it out, but they were not able to move it. The mother helped them, but it was of no use. Then all the brothers rose up, they left their mother to watch, and set out to seek him who had shot the arrow. Ghvthisavari bethought himself, and set out; he followed the flight of the arrow to see where it had fallen.

He went on and on until he came to the devis' house. He looked in and saw in the middle a fire burning, in which stuck his arrow. He went in, and was about to draw the arrow out when the devis' mother cried: 'Who art thou, wretch, who darest to venture here? Art you not afraid that I shall eat you?' 'You shalt not eat me,' said Ghvthisavari, drawing out his arrow and hurling it at the old woman. He cut her into a hundred pieces, gave her to the dogs, and told them to throw her into the sea. He lay down in the devis' house and rested.

The devis wandered far and wide in their search, but nowhere could they learn any tidings of him they sought. Then they said: 'Perhaps some one will enter our house and steal, while we are here. Let one of us go home, and the rest watch here.' Each wished to go, and promised to run back again as quickly as possible. But the devis chose the two-headed brother, and sent him.

The two-headed brother came, and saw that his mother was no longer there, but in her place was a strange youth. He clapped him on the shoulder, and cried out: 'Who art thou, wretch, who darest to venture here? For fear of me, bird cannot fly under heaven, nor can ant crawl on earth. Art you not afraid that I shall eat you?' 'You shalt not eat me,' said Ghvthisavari, throwing an arrow. He cut him into a hundred pieces, gave him to the dogs, and made them throw him into the sea.

The four remaining devis waited for their two-headed brother, but he did not come. They thought that perhaps he was staying eating him who had shot the arrow, so they sent the three-headed brother.

The three-headed devi came home, and found neither his mother nor brother, and called out: 'For fear of me bird cannot fly in air, nor can ant creep on earth. Who art you who darest to venture here? Art you not afraid that I shall eat you?' 'You shalt not eat me,' said Ghvthisavari, casting an arrow. He cut him into a hundred pieces, gave him to the dogs, and made them throw him into the sea.

The remaining brothers waited and waited, and then sent the five-headed devi. He too boasted, but Ghvthisavari did unto him that day even as he had done unto the others. Then the nine-headed devi went. The same thing befell him as his brothers.

The ten-headed devi was now the only one left. He thought to himself: 'My brothers are probably eating, and will not leave anything for me.' He rose and went too.

He went in and saw that his mother and brothers were not there. Instead, there was a strange youth, lying down resting. The devi called out: 'From fear of me the bird in heaven dare not fly, on earth the ant dare not crawl. Who art you who darest to venture here? Art you not afraid that I shall eat you?' 'You shalt not eat me,' said Ghvthisavari, throwing an arrow and killing him. He drew out his sword, cut off his heads, and gave him to the dogs to throw into the sea.

Ghvthisavari was left master of the field. Then he said to himself: 'I will go and bring my mother and her companion here, and I shall live as I like.' He went forth and brought them, settled them in the house, and prepared for the chase.

From the sea there staggered forth the last ten-headed devi, and hid under a tree. When Ghvthisavari had cut off his heads, in his haste he had left the tenth on. Now, it was in this head that the soul was placed, so the devi came out on to the shore, full of wrath.

The next day Ghvthisavari again went out hunting. His mother, wishing to see the surroundings, went out of the house into the garden. As she walked about, the devi suddenly appeared at the foot of a tree. The devi pleaded, saying: 'Do not give me up! Do not tell you son that I am hidden here!' Ghvthisavari's mother promised, and when Ghvthisavari went out to the chase, his mother always took food and drink to the devi. And at last she loved him.

Once the devi said to her: 'Why should we live thus? We see each other only in secret, I am continually in terror of you son. Go home now, lie down in bed and pretend to be ill. When you son comes home and asks you what is the matter, say to him: "Go to such and such a place and bring me some pieces of stag's horns as a remedy." When you son goes to the stag, it will butt him with its horns, and then you and I shall remain here alone.'

The woman agreed to this plan, went in and lay down in her bed. Ghvthisavari came home, and seeing his mother sick, he said to her: 'What is the matter? Tell me what will cure you, and I will find it, even if it be bird's milk.' His mother said: 'If you can bring to me a piece of such and such a stag's horn, from a certain place, I shall be well; if not, I shall die.' Ghvthisavari slung his bow and arrows over his shoulders, took his dogs and set out.

When he had gone some way, he came to an immense wide plain, where he saw a stag feeding. It had such large horns that they reached to heaven.

He sat down and took an arrow. Just as he was about to let it fly, the stag made a sign, and cried out: 'Ghvthisavari! Ghvthisavari! why shoot me? What have I done to deserve this of you? Dost you not know that you mother has deceived you. She seeks you ruin, therefore has she sent you here. Behold, here is a piece of my horn, take it, and here is one of my hairs, take it with you also, and when you art in trouble, think of me, and I shall be there.' Ghvthisavari thanked the stag joyfully, and went away.

He went home with the stag's horn to his mother. She took it, and thanked him.

The next day Ghvthisavari again went to the chase. His mother immediately hastened to the devi and said: 'Ghvthisavari has returned unharmed, and has brought the stag's horn.' 'Well,' said the devi, 'pretend to be ill as before, and tell him that he must bring a wild boar's bristle from such and such a place, else there is no cure for you.'

The woman ran in, lay down in bed, and began to moan. Ghvthisavari returned, and seeing his mother ill, he asked her: 'What is this, mother? What aileth you? Tell me what will cure you, and even bird's milk I will not leave unfound.' 'If you wilt seek in such and such a place, and bring me a bristle from a certain wild boar, then all will be well, but if not, I shall die.' 'May you Ghvthisavari die if he does not find this!' said Ghvthisavari, slinging his bow and arrows on his shoulders, and taking his dogs, he set forth on the quest.

He went a long way, and came into a wood. There he found a boar's lair, but boar was there none. He went on a little, and saw another lair, but again there was no boar in it. He went away once more, and saw the boar itself. It had changed its lair twice, and now lay in a third. Ghvthisavari approached it, took aim with an arrow, but, as he was about to let it fly, the boar cried out: 'Ghvthisavari! Ghvthisavari! What have I done to harm you? Why kill me? Dost you not know that you mother has deceived you? She wishes for you death, therefore has she sent you here. But since you wouldst like a bristle, pull out as many as you wishest, and take them with you.' Ghvthisavari came up, took a bristle, and was going away, when the boar took out a hair, gave it to him, and said: 'Here is also a hair for you; when you art in trouble remember me, and I shall come to you.' Ghvthisavari took the hair, thanked the boar, and went away.

He came home, gave his mother the bristle, and again hastened out to the chase. His mother ran immediately to the devi, and said complainingly: 'Ghvthisavari has returned unharmed, and has brought me the boar's bristle.' The devi replied: 'Then go, again, pretend to be ill, and say to Ghvthisavari: "If you will go to a certain place, where a certain griffin lives, and bring me the flesh of its young, I shall be well; if not, I shall die." You know he cannot do that, and you and I shall stay here together.'

The woman rejoiced, ran quickly back to bed, and began to moan. Ghvthisavari came in, saw his mother in bed, and asked the cause. His mother replied as the devi had commanded. Ghvthisavari answered: 'Then may Ghvthisavari die if he find not what you wish.' He went away.

He went on and on, and at last came to a plain, where stood a very big tree, whose top stretched to heaven. On a branch there was a nest, from which fledglings peeped out. Then, from far away in the sky, there appeared a huge, strange bird, something like an eagle. It swooped down, and just as it was about to seize the young birds, Ghvthisavari drew his bow, and killed it. Just then appeared the griffin, mother of the young ones. She thought Ghvthisavari her enemy, and was about to seize him, but her fledglings cried out that he had killed the bird that would have drunk their blood, and had saved them.

Although the griffin did not bring up more than three birds in a year, yet she was in constant terror until they had learnt to fly, because this same bird used to seize and eat them.

When she learnt that Ghvthisavari had killed their cruel enemy, she came to him, and said: 'Tell me what you wishest? why art you come here? and I will immediately satisfy you desire.' Ghvthisavari said: 'I have a mother who is ill; unless I take her young griffin's flesh she will die.' The griffin said in reply: 'You mother deceives you, and is not ill at all; she seeks you death. Here are my fledglings, if you wantest them, but do not kill them, take them with you alive.' She pulled out a feather, and gave it to him, saying: 'Take this with you, and when you art in trouble think of me, and I shall be there.' Ghvthisavari thanked her heartily, took away a fledgling, and went home.

He came in, gave the young griffin to his mother, who said: 'Now, my child, I am quite well, and shall want nothing else,' and she sent him away. Ghvthisavari went out hunting. The woman went out hastily to the devi, and complained, saying: 'Ghvthisavari has brought the fledgling, and he himself has returned alive.' The devi was very angry, but calmed down and said: 'When Ghvthisavari comes in, tell him he must be bathed, and when he sits down in the tub, put a cover over him and call for me. I will come and hammer down the lid, and throw him into the sea.' The woman rejoiced at this plan, went in and heated water. When Ghvthisavari came in, his mother said: 'Come, child, I will bathe you, it is some time since you wert bathed.' Ghvthisavari did not like this, but at last he consented. He sat down in the tub, his mother shut the lid, and called the devi. The devi ran in and hammered down the lid. Then he lifted the tub up and rolled it into the sea.

Ghvthisavari's dogs saw this; they went to the edge of the water and barked. They barked until the very stones might have been moved with pity. Then they said: 'Let us go and seek his friends, they may perchance help us.' Four remained and four went to seek his friends. They came to the stag, then to the boar, and then to the griffin. These all arose and immediately went to the water's edge.

They thought and planned, and at last decided what to do. They said to the griffin: 'Fly up high, strike and cleave the water with you wings, the tub will appear, the stag will throw it on to the shore with its horns; then the boar will strike with his tusk, the tub will break, and Ghvthisavari will come forth.' They all did as they were told.

The griffin flew up high in the air, beat with its wings as hard as it could; it cleft the sea into three. The tub was seen, and the stag did not let it fall, but threw it with its horns, and let it down on the shore. Then the boar struck it, crying out: 'Ghvthisavari, lie down in the bottom!' He struck with his tusk, broke the tub, and Ghvthisavari came forth unharmed.

After this the friends went away, each to his own home, Ghvthisavari remained thinking. Just then a ragged swineherd came along. Ghvthisavari said to this swineherd: 'Come, give me you clothes, and I will put them on.' The swineherd was afraid, and thought: 'This stranger will take my coat and not give me his,' and he ran away. Ghvthisavari pursued him, took off his clothes, and put them on himself; he gave the man his coat, left with him his dogs, and went away.

He came home as if he were a beggar, and asked alms of his mother. When the devi saw him, he looked ferociously at him, and said: 'Go back to where you came from, unless I do to you as you deserve.'

Just then Ghvthisavari saw his bow and arrow in the corner, and cried out: 'We shall see who goes hence! I am Ghvthisavari!' Saying this he drew his bow, shot first the devi and then his mother, killing them both. Then he went to the companion, scolded her well for not warning him, and killed her too. He went away, brought his dogs, and returned to the house to rest.

There came then, no one knows whence, a certain youth; he saw his father, mother, and their servant were all killed, and asked Ghvthisavari to fight. He was Ghvthisavari's mother's son by the devi; Ghvthisavari did not know this, and came to the combat. A long time they struggled, a long time they strove, but neither could strike the other. Then Ghvthisavari said: 'Come, friend, let us each tell the other his story, and afterwards we can fight.' 'Good!' 'Very well,' they said, and each told his tale.

When Ghvthisavari learnt that this was his own brother, he said: 'It is indeed fortunate that we told our tales first, for if we had killed each other there would have been no help for it.' After this the two brothers went into the house, and they lived happily together.

Once Ghvthisavari said to his younger brother: 'Let us go, brother, and seek our fortunes, we shall become like old women if we live thus.' 'I am willing,' replied the younger; so they set out.

They wandered on until they came to a place where two roads met. One led to the right and one to the left. In the middle of the roads stood a stone pillar, on which was written: 'Whoever goes to the left will come back, but he who goes to the right will never return.' Ghvthisavari took the road to the right and his brother went to the left. Ghvthisavari said: 'Know that if the water on the roof changes into blood I shall be in trouble. Come then to my aid. If the water on my roof turns into blood, I shall come and help you in you trouble.' Then they divided the dogs: each took four, said farewell, and set out.

Ghvthisavari went on until he came to the shore of a sea, so vast that the eye could not measure it. Twelve men were on this side, twelve on that. Whoever comes to this sea must jump over; if he leaps over without wetting his feet he may marry the king's daughter, who is very beautiful; if not, he is drowned in the sea; and whoever dares not jump at all is seized by the sentinels, and taken before the king.

Ghvthisavari came, and the sentinels told him the conditions. Ghvthisavari took a spring with all his might and main, and leaped over so that not a drop of water touched him. He saw the other sentinels, and they told him that they must take him before the king. When the king saw him he rejoiced, and gave him his fair daughter to wife.

That night Ghvthisavari asked his wife: 'Where is the best hunting to be had in the kingdom?' She replied: 'If you goest to the left you wilt return; if you goest to the right you wilt never return.' The next morning Ghvthisavari arose at daybreak, took his bow and arrow, and went to the right hand.

He shot an arrow and killed a hare, he tied its feet and left it; he shot another arrow and killed a stag, he bound its feet together and left it too. He shot a third arrow, and it stuck in a burning fire.

He went on and on until he reached this fire. Then he killed a stag, put it on the fire, and sat down at the side. He roasted meat, ate some, and gave some to his dogs. Behold, no one knows from where, a toothless old woman appeared. She begged Ghvthisavari to give her something to eat. He did so; he ate, but the old woman ate ten times more. For every mouthful Ghvthisavari took she took a basketful. Ghvthisavari looked on in amazement. The old woman finished all the food. Then she took a little stone and threw it at Ghvthisavari's bow and arrow. They turned into stone, and fell on the ground. Then she took the little stone and threw it at the dogs, who also became petrified. She took them one by one in her hand and swallowed them. Ghvthisavari was stupefied; he seized his bow and arrow to kill the old woman, but he could not move it; it fell to earth. Then the old woman turned her stone towards Ghvthisavari, who lost his strength, and became as a corpse. The old woman lifted him up in her hand and swallowed him. At that moment the water changed to blood, and the younger brother knew that Ghvthisavari had fallen into misfortune, and set out to help him.

When he had gone some way he came to the water's edge, on each side of which stood the twelve sentinels. He leaped across. The sentinels were surprised, they thought it was Ghvthisavari, and asked him whence he came and where he was going. The youth told them nothing, and did not let them know who he was. He came to the king. That night he was given his brother's wife, but when he lay down he put a sword between them, and did not touch her. Then he asked her: 'Where is the best hunting?' She replied: 'If you goest to the left you will return, if to the right you wilt never return. Do not go; did I not tell you the same thing yesterday?' 'I asked you, and I went one way, but did not like it; now I ask you again,' said the youth. He rose the next morning, and went to the right hand.

When he had gone a little way he saw the dead hare with its feet bound; he went on farther and saw the dead stag with its feet bound. He said to himself: 'My brother must have come this way; this is some of the game he has killed.' He again went on, and saw the fire burning. Beside it lay Ghvthisavari's bow and arrow, and he said to himself: 'Here my brother has met his fate.' Then he killed some game and roasted it on the fire.

There appeared, no one knows whence, the same old woman. She sat down and waited for her share of roast meat. In eating, the old woman's behaviour was the same as before. When she had finished the food she was still hungry. She took a little stone, and lifted it to throw at the dogs. The youth thought to himself: 'It must have been in this way that this old woman swallowed my brother Ghvthisavari.' He seized the old woman by the throat, cleft her breast open, and took out Ghvthisavari and his dogs. Then he killed the old woman and poured her blood over Ghvthisavari, the dogs, and the bow and arrow. Ghvthisavari and his dogs came back to life, and the bow and arrow were raised from the earth. When Ghvthis-avari woke to consciousness he said: 'Ugh! I have had such a dream.' Then his brother said: 'You hast not dreamt'; and he told him what had happened.

Ghvthisavari rejoiced, and they both went to their new kinsman, the king. On the way, Ghvthisavari was very melancholy, for he thought that his brother must have married his wife. His brother looked at him and said: 'May this arrow strike me on the part of my body that has touched you wife, and kill me.' Thus spoke Ghvthisavari's brother, and threw up an arrow. It fell, struck him in the little finger, and he died. Ghvthisavari left his brother, went in, and, when he had learnt all, was deeply grieved. He went, no one knows where, found immortal water, and brought his brother back to life. Then he found him a fair wife, and they dwelt together, happy in fraternal affection and in love.

THE HERMIT
PHILOSOPHER

There was once a great philosopher who had acquired all the branches of wisdom. He abandoned the world and went far away into the wilderness. There he lived alone and prayed. And there were six other philosophers, men of great learning, lovers of knowledge. They disputed about some word, and none of them could solve the question. So they set out to seek the solitary sage and asked him about the difficult word, but he did not answer them for a long time. They asked him again, and he said: "You have spent all your substance in studying to speak much; I have left my household, and the world, that I may live in silence and not speak at all." He did not utter another word, so they went back ashamed and unanswered.

THE SERPENT AND
THE PEASANT

There was once a happy king. Great or small, maid or man, every one was happy in his kingdom, every one was joyful and glad.

Once this monarch saw a vision. In his dream there hung from the ceiling in his house a fox suspended by the tail. He awoke, he could not see what the dream signified. He assembled his viziers, but they also could not divine what this dream presaged.

Then he said: 'Assemble all my kingdom together, perhaps some one may interpret it.' On the third day all the people of his kingdom assembled in the king's palace. Among others came a poor peasant.

In one place he had to travel along a footpath. The path on both sides was shut in by rocky mountains. When the peasant arrived there, he saw a serpent lying on the path, stretching its neck and putting out its tongue.

When the peasant went near, the serpent called out: 'Good day, where art you going, peasant?' The peasant told what was the matter. The serpent said: 'Do not fear him, give me you word that what the king gives, you wilt share with me, and I will teach you.' The peasant rejoiced, gave his word, and swore, saying: 'I will bring you all that the king presents to me if you wilt aid me in this matter.' The serpent said: 'I shall divide it in halves, half will be yours; when you seest the king, say: "The fox meant this, that in the kingdom there is cunning, hypocrisy, and treachery."'

The peasant went, he approached the king, and told even what the serpent had taught. The king was very much pleased, and gave great presents. The peasant did not return by that way, so that he might not share with the serpent, but went by another path.

Some time passed by, the king saw another vision: in his dream a naked sword hung suspended from the roof. The king this time sent a man quickly for the peasant, and asked him to come. The peasant was very uneasy in mind. There was nothing for it, the peasant went by the same footpath as before.

He came to that place where he saw the serpent before, but now he saw the serpent there no more. He cried out: 'O serpent, come here one moment, I need you.' He ceased not until the serpent came. It said: 'What do you want? what distresses you?' The peasant answered: 'Thus and thus is the matter, and I should like some aid.' The serpent replied: 'Go, tell the king that the naked sword means war--now enemies are intriguing within and without; he must prepare for battle and attack.'

The peasant thanked the serpent and went. He came and told the king even as the serpent had commanded. The king was pleased, he began to prepare for war, and gave the peasant great presents. Now the peasant went by that path where the serpent was waiting. The serpent said: 'Now give me the half you hast promised.' The peasant replied: 'Half, certainly not! I shall give you a black stone and a burning cinder.' He drew out his sword and pursued it. The serpent retreated into a hole, but the peasant followed it, and cut off its tail with his sword.

Some time passed, and the king again saw a vision. In this vision a slain sheep was hanging from the roof. The king sent a man quickly for the peasant. The peasant was now very much afraid. And he said: 'How can I approach the king?'

Formerly the serpent had taught him, but now it could no longer do this; for its goodness he had wounded it with the sword.

Nevertheless, he went by that footpath. When he came to the place where the serpent had been, he cried out: 'O serpent, come here one moment, I want to ask you something.' The serpent came. The man told his grief. The serpent said: 'If you givest me half of what the king gives you, I shall tell you.' He promised and swore. The serpent said: 'This is a sign that now everywhere peace falls on all, the people are become like quiet, gentle sheep.'

The peasant thanked it, and went his way. When he came to the king, he spoke as the serpent had instructed him. The king was exceedingly pleased, and gave him greater presents. The peasant returned by the way where the serpent was waiting. He came to the serpent, divided everything he had received from the king, and said: 'You hast been patient with me, and now I will give you even what was given me before by the king.' He humbly asked forgiveness for his former offences. The serpent said: 'Be not grieved nor troubled; it certainly was not your fault. The first time, when all the people were entirely deceitful, and there was treachery and hypocrisy in the land, you too wert a deceiver, for, in spite of you promise, you went home by another way. The second time, when there was war everywhere, quarrels and assassination, thou, too, didst quarrel with me, and cut off my tail. But now, when peace and love have fallen on all, you bring the gifts, and share all with me. Go, brother, may the peace of God rest with you! I do not want your wealth.' And the serpent went away and cast itself into its hole.

GULAMBARA AND
SULAMBARA

One upon a time, there was a blind monarch, who all the doctors in the kingdom could not cure.

At last one doctor said: 'In a certain sea is a fish red as blood. If this is caught, killed, and its blood sprinkled on your eyes, it may do good—the light will come back into your eyes—if not, there can be no other cure for you.'

Then the king assembled every fisherman in his realm, and commanded: 'Go wherever it may be or may not be, catch such a fish as this, and I shall give you a rich reward.'

Some time passed by. An old fisherman caught just such a crimson fish, and took it to the king. The king was asleep, and they did not dare to wake him, so they put the fish into a basin full of water.

Just then his son returned from his lessons. He saw the blood-red fish swimming in the basin. He took it up in his hands, caressed it, and said: 'What do you want with the pretty fish in the basin?' They said to him: 'This is good for your father, it must be killed, its blood sprinkled on his eyes, and he will regain his sight.' 'But is it not a sin to kill it?' asked the prince; and he took the fish out to a stream in the meadow, and gave it freedom.

A little while after, the king awoke; his viziers said to him: 'An old fisherman brought to you a blood-red fish, but your son, who had just returned from his lessons, let it away.'

The king was very angry, and sent his son from the house. 'Go, I shall be well when you are no longer remembered in the kingdom; with my eyes I cannot look upon you, but never let me hear yours unpleasant voice again.' The boy was grieved, rose, and went away.

He went, he went, and he knew not where he went. On the way he saw a stream. He was weary and sat down to rest on the bank. Behold, a boy of his own age came out of the water. He came to the prince, greeted him, and said: 'Where did you come from? And what troubles you?' The prince went to him and told him all that had happened to him. His new acquaintance said: 'I also am discontented with my lot, so let us become brothers, and live together.' The prince agreed, and they went on their way.

They travelled on some distance, when they came to a town, and they dwelt there. When the next day dawned, his adopted brother said to the prince: 'Stay you at home, do not go out of doors, lest they eat you, for such is the custom here.' The prince promised, and from morning until night he sat indoors. The other boy was away in the town all day. At twilight, when he came home, he had a handkerchief quite full of provisions.

Several days slipped by. The prince stayed in all day, and his brother brought the food and drink. At last the prince said to himself: 'This is shameful! My adopted brother goes out and brings in food and drink. Why do I not do something? What an idle fellow I am! I will go and do something!'

And so it happened that one day the king's son went into the town; he wandered here and there, and in one place saw his brother, who was sitting cross-legged on the ground, at his feet was stretched a pocket handkerchief, in his hand he held a chonguri[2], which he played, and he chanted to it with a sweet voice. Whoever passed by placed money in the handkerchief.

The king's son listened and listened, and said: 'No, this

---

2 A chonguri is a Georgian string instrument.

must not be; this is not my business.' So he turned and went back.

Near there he saw a tower. Outside was a wall, and on the top were arranged in rows men's heads: some were quite shriveled up, some had an unpleasant odor of decay, and some had just been placed there.

He looked and looked, and could not understand what it meant. He asked a man: 'Whose tower is this, and why are men's heads arranged in rows in this way?' He was told: 'In this tower dwells a maiden beautiful as the sun. Any king's son may ask her in marriage. She asks him a question: if he cannot answer it his head is cut off, but if he can he may demand her in marriage. No one has yet been able to answer her question.'

The prince thought and thought, and said to himself: 'I will go. I will ask this maiden in marriage: I will know if this is my fate. What is to be will be. What can she ask me that I shall not know?' So he rose and went.

He came to the sunlike maiden and asked her in marriage. She answered: 'It is well, but first I have a question to ask you; if you can answer, then I am yours, if not, I shall cut off your head.' 'So let it be,' said the prince. 'I ask you this, Who are Gulambara and Sulambara?' enquired the beautiful maiden. The king's son said to himself: 'I know indeed that Gulambara and Sulambara are names of flowers, but I never heard in all my life of human beings thus named.' He asked three days grace and went away.

He went home and told his brother what had happened, and said: 'If you cannot help me now, in three days I shall lose my head.' His brother reproached him, saying: 'Did I not tell you to stay indoors? This is a wicked town.' But then he comforted him, saying: 'Go now, buy a pennyworth of aromatic gum and a candle. I have a grandmother, I shall take you to her, and she will help you. But at the moment when my grandmother looks at us, give her the gum and the candle, or she will eat you.'

He bought the gum and the candle, and they set out. The grandmother was standing in her doorway; the prince immediately gave her the gum and the candle. 'What is it? What is the matter with you?' enquired the grandmother of the prince's adopted brother. He came forward, and told everything in detail. Then he added: 'This is my good brother, and certainly you should help him.' 'Very well,' said the old woman to the prince; 'sit down on my back.' The prince seated himself on her back. The old woman flew up high, and then, in the twinkling of an eye, she flew down into the depths.

She took him into a town there, and went to the entrance of a bazaar. She pointed out a shopkeeper and said: 'Go and engage yourself as assistant to this shopkeeper; but in the evening, when he leaves business and goes home, tell him that he must take you with him, and must not leave you in the shop. Where you go with him you wilt learn the story of Gulambara and Sulambara. Then when you have need of me, whistle and I shall be there.'

The prince did exactly as the old woman had instructed him; he went to the butcher, as his assistant. At twilight, when the butcher spoke of going home, the prince said to him: 'Do not leave me here; I am a stranger in this land. I am afraid; take me with you.' The butcher objected strongly, but the prince entreated him until he agreed.

The butcher went home, and took the prince with him. They came to a wall, opened a door, went in, and it closed. Inside that, was another wall; they went through that, and it closed. They passed thus through nine walls, and then they entered a house. The butcher opened a cupboard door, took out a woman's head, and then an iron whip. He put down the decaying head and struck it. He struck and struck until the head was completely gone.

When the prince saw this he was astonished, and enquired: 'Tell me, why do you strike this head that is so mutilated, and whose head is this?' The butcher made answer: 'I tell this to no one, this is my secret, but if I do tell any one he must then lose his head.' 'I still wish to know,' said the prince. The butcher rose, took a sword, prepared himself, and said to the prince. 'I had a wife who was so lovely that she excelled the sun; her name was Gulambara. I kept her under these nine locks, and I took care of her so that not even the wind of heaven blew on her. Whatever she asked me I gave her at once. I loved her to distraction, and trusted her, and she told me that she loved no one in the world but me. At that time I had an assistant who was called Sulambara, and my wife loved him and deceived me. Once I found them together, and seized them. I locked one in one cupboard and the other in another. Whenever I came home from business I went to the cupboards, and took out first one and then the other, and beat them as hard as I could. I struck so hard that Sulambara crumbled away yesterday, and only Gulambara's head remained, and that has just now crumbled away before yours eyes.'

The story ended, he took his sword and said to the prince: 'Now I am going to fulfill my threat, so come here and I shall cut off you head.' The prince entreated him: 'Give me a little time. I will go to the door and pray to my God, and then do to me even as you wish.' The butcher thought: 'It can do no harm to let him go to the door for a short time, for he certainly cannot open the nine doors; let him pray to his God and have his wish.'

The prince went to the gate and whistled. Immediately the old woman flew down, took him on her back, and flew off. The youth went to the town where the beautiful maiden dwelt, and told the sunlike one the story of Gulambara and Sulambara. The maiden was very much surprised; when she had heard all, she agreed to marry him. They were married; she collected all her worldly possessions, and set out with the prince for his father's kingdom.

When he came to the brook, his adopted brother appeared before him, and said: 'In you trouble I befriended you, and now, when you are happy, shall this friendship cease? Whatever you hast obtained has been by my counsel, therefore you should share it with me.' The prince divided everything in halves, but still his adopted brother was not pleased. 'It is all very well to share this with me, while you have the beautiful maiden.' The prince arose and gave up his own share of the goods.

His adopted brother would not take it, and spoke thus: 'If you holdest fast to our friendship you shouldst share with me this maiden, the most precious of you possessions!' As he said this he seized the maiden's hand, bound her to a tree, stretched forth his sword, and, as he was about to strike, a green stream flowed from the terror-stricken maiden's mouth. Again the youth raised his sword. The same thing happened. A third time he prepared to strike, with the same result. Then he came, unbound her from the tree, gave her to the prince, and said: 'Although this maiden was beautiful, yet she was venomous, and, sooner or later, would have killed you. Now whatever poison was in her is completely gone, so do not fear her in the slightest degree. Go! And God guide you. As for these possessions, they are yours; I do not want them. May God give you His peace.' From his pocket he took out a handkerchief, gave it to the prince, and said: 'Take this handkerchief with you; when you reachest home wipe your father's eyes with it and he will see. I am the fish that was in the basin, and you set me free. Know, then, that kindness of heart is never lost.' So saying, the prince's adopted brother disappeared.

The prince remained astonished. Before he had time to express his gratitude the young man had suddenly disappeared. At last, when he had recovered himself, he took his wife and went to his father. He laid the handkerchief on the king's eyes, and his sight came back to him. When he saw his only son and his beautiful daughter-in-law his joy was so great that his eyes filled with tears. His son sat down and told him all that had happened since he left him.

THE TWO BROTHERS

Once upon a time there were two brothers. Each of them possessed ten loaves of bread; and they said: 'Let us go and seek our fortune.' So they arose and went forth.

When they had gone a little way they were hungry. One brother said to the other: 'Come, let us eat you bread first, then we can eat mine.' And he agreed, and they took of his loaves and did eat, and they afterwards went on their way.

And they travelled for some time in this manner. At last, when these ten loaves were finished, the brother who had first spoken said: 'Now, my brother, you can go you way and I shall go mine. You hast no loaves left, and I will not let you eat my bread.' So saying, he left him to continue his journey alone.

He went on and on, and came to a mill in a thick forest. He saw the miller and said: 'For the love of God, let me stay here to-night.' The miller answered: 'Brother, it is a very terrible thing to be here at night; as you see, even I go elsewhere. Presently wild beasts will assemble in the wood, and probably come here.' 'Have no fear for me; I shall stay here. The beasts cannot kill me,' answered the boy. The miller tried to persuade him not to endanger his life, but when he found his arguments were of no avail he rose and went home. The boy crept inside the hopper of the mill.

There appeared, from no one knows where, a big bear; he was followed by a wolf, then a jackal; and they all made a great noise in the mill. They leaped and bounded just as if they were having a dance. He was terrified, and, trembling from fear, he lay down, quaking all over, in the hopper. At last the bear said: 'Come, let each of us tell something he has seen or heard.' 'We shall tell our tales, but you must begin,' cried his companions. The bear said: 'Well, on a hill that I know dwells a mouse. This mouse has a great heap of money, which it spreads out when the sun shines. If any one knew of this mouse's hole, and went there on a sunny day, when the money is spread out, and struck the mouse with a twig, and killed it, he would become possessed of great wealth.'

'That is not wonderful!' said the wolf. 'I know a certain town where there is no water, and every mouthful has to be carried a great distance, and an enormous price is paid for it! The inhabitants do not know that in the centre of their town, under a certain stone, is beautiful, pure water. Now, if any one knew of this, and would roll away that stone, he would obtain great wealth.'

'That is nothing,' said the jackal. 'I know of a king who has one only daughter, and she has been an invalid for three years. Quite a simple remedy would cure her: if she were bathed in a bath of beech leaves she would be healed. You have no idea what a fortune any one would get if he only knew this.'

When they had spoken thus, day began to dawn. The bear, the wolf, and the jackal went away into the wood. The boy came out of the hopper, gave thanks to God, and went to the mouse's hole, of which the bear had spoken.

He arrived, and saw that the story was true. There was the mouse with the money spread out. He snuck up noiselessly, and, taking twigs in his hand, he struck the mouse until he had killed it, and then gathered up the money. Then he went to the waterless town, rolled away the stone, and behold! Streams of water flowed forth. He received a reward for this, and set out for the kingdom of which the jackal had spoken. He arrived, and enquired of the king: 'What wilt you give me if I cure you daughter?' The king replied: 'If you can do this

I will give you my daughter to wife.' The youth prepared the remedy, made the princess bathe in it, and she was cured. The king rejoiced greatly, gave him the maiden in marriage, and appointed him heir to the kingdom.

This story reached the ears of the youth's brother. He went on and on, and it came to pass that he found his brother. He asked him: 'How and by what cunning has this happened?' The fortunate youth told him all in detail. 'I also shall go and stay at that mill a night or two.' His brother used many entreaties to dissuade him, and when he would not listen, said: 'Well, go if you wilt, but I warn you again it is very dangerous.' However, he would not be persuaded, and went away. He crept into the hopper, and was there all night.

From some place or other arrived the former guests--the bear, the wolf, and the jackal. The bear said: 'That day when I told you my story the mouse was killed, and the money all taken away.' The wolf said: 'And the stone was rolled away in the waterless town of which I spoke.' 'And the king's daughter was cured,' added the jackal. 'Then perhaps some one was listening when we talked here,' said the bear. 'Perhaps some one is here now,' shrieked his companions. 'Then let us go and look; certainly no one shall listen again,' said the three; and they looked in all the corners. They sought and sought everywhere. At last the bear looked into the hopper, and saw the trembling boy. He dragged him out and tore him to pieces.

THE PRINCE

There was once a king who had great possessions, but his wife had no children, and he was a prey to grief.

One day when he was very melancholy a courtier came to him and said: 'Most mighty monarch! you hast no son, and you givest no gifts; what will you subjects think of you? What wilt you do with this wealth stored up by you?' The king took these words to heart; the next day he gave a great feast, and scattered alms lavishly.

From no one knows where there appeared at that time an old woman. She came to the king and said: 'What wilt you give me if I bring you a son?' The king replied: 'Whatever you askest of me, that will I give you.' The old woman drew forth from her pocket an apple, which she cut in three and gave to the king, saying, 'Let you wife eat this, and she will have three children; but, remember, I shall come back in seven years and you must give me you youngest son.' The king consented, gave his wife the apple, and she ate it.

Some time passed, and the queen bore three sons, and the youngest was the most beautiful of all. The king could not bear to think that he must give him up. He said to himself: 'I shall put him behind nine locks, and when the old woman comes, I shall tell her that my youngest son is dead, but that she can take the two elder if she wishes.'

After seven years the old woman came, and demanded of the king his youngest son. He did just as he had planned. He locked up his youngest son behind nine locks, and said to the old woman: 'My youngest son is dead, but here are the other two, take them.' The old woman would not believe him. She searched every corner of the palace, opened the nine locks, and took away the young prince. She went homeward, and took him with her.

When they had gone a little way, they came to a brook where they found an old woman washing dirty linen. When she saw the beautiful prince she called him back, and said sadly to him: 'Dost you know you art being led into misfortune? Why dost you go with that witch? You certainly can not escape alive from her hands!' When the prince heard this, he went to the witch and said: 'Let me go and have a word with this old woman. I shall overtake you in a minute.' The witch let him go.

The prince went back to his own home, filled a cup with water, and placed it near the fire. Having done this, he said: 'When that water changes to blood, I shall be dead, but as long as it is pure I shall be alive.' Then he went away, quickly overtook the witch, and they went on together.

At last they arrived in a dark ravine; the home of the witch was there in a rocky cave. In the house she had three daughters and two horses--one for herself and one for her daughters. The old woman went in, entrusted the prince to her daughters' care, and fell asleep.

Now this old witch had a habit of sleeping for seven days and nights, and it was impossible to rouse her.

When her daughters saw the prince they admired him very much, and said: 'It is a shame that so handsome a boy should be destroyed! Come, our mother shall not have him to eat; we must help him to escape in some way.' 'We will!' cried the sisters; and they thought of a plan of escape.

The eldest sister gave him her comb, and said: 'When my mother overtakes you, throw this behind you and hasten on; a thick forest will spring up between you and my mother, who will have difficulty in passing through it.'

The second sister gave him a pair of scissors, and said: 'When my mother overtakes you, throw these scissors behind you—jagged rocks, hard as adamant, will rise between you and my mother, who will have difficulty in crossing them, but hasten you on.'

The youngest sister gave him a lump of salt, and said: 'When my mother overtakes you, throw this behind you--between you will roll a sea, which my mother will never cross.' Then they carefully saddled their own steed, gave the youth everything he wanted, and sent him away. He thanked them heartily and set out.

Seven days passed. The witch awoke, and looked for her dinner, but it was no longer there. She went to her steed and enquired of it, 'Shall we eat bread or shall we set out at once?' 'Whether we eat bread or not we cannot overtake him,' said the steed to the witch. She did not abandon her intention, but, having eaten bread, mounted her horse and set off in pursuit of the prince.

After riding some distance she overtook him. The prince looked back, and, seeing the old woman approach, drew the comb from his pocket and threw it down behind him. Between them, there rose a forest so thick that even a fly could not go through it. The old woman was annoyed and hindered, but at last, in some way or other, she passed through it.

When she reached the open country she spurred her horse on with might and main, and again approached the prince, who looked behind and saw the old woman. He took the scissors from his pocket, and threw them down. Between them appeared a jagged rock, hard as steel, so that no iron could cut it; the horse cut its feet, and, not being able to go any further, fell down; yet the old woman would not give in. She jumped from the horse's back and went forward on foot. She passed the rocks, reached the plain again, and hastened on.

She flew over the ground as if she had wings. The prince looked back, and saw how near the old woman was. He took the piece of salt from his pocket, and threw it behind him. There flowed between them a sea so vast that no bird could cross it. The old woman was not daunted, even by this, she waded into the sea, determined to cross it, but she was drowned.

The prince often looked behind, but he could no longer see the old woman. Then his heart was filled with joy, and he went on gaily. He himself knew not where he went. He grew hungrier and hungrier, until he was ravenous.

At last he saw a fire: he went up, and there was burning a huge fire, over which hung a kettle of arrack, and food cooking; around it lay nine devis, who were brothers. They were fast asleep, but there was a lame one watching as sentinel. The prince did not wait to ask leave of the devis; he came up, lifted the pot off the fire, took some food, and when he had eaten, put the pot back. He then lay down and began to snore loudly. The lame devi looked on with amazement from a distance.

A short time afterwards a devi awoke. He looked round and saw a human being sleeping there. He said joyfully: 'This will be a dainty morsel for us,' and went towards the boy. But the lame devi followed him and said: 'Leave him alone, lay not a hand upon him; he is to be feared—just now he took our pot from the fire, ate some food, and placed it on the fire again; he has done alone what is difficult for us ten.' The devi thought better of it, and turned away.

A second devi then rose and did the same, but the lame devi prevented him. As each devi awoke he went to the boy, but the lame devi took care of them.

When all the devis were roused and had begun to eat, the prince woke up too. He came to the devis and asked them to swear brotherhood. The devis said: 'Who art thou, who art so courageous? What brought you here?' The prince answered: 'I was hungry, I saw the fire and I came to the fire.' Then the devis said: 'Very well, if you wishest us to swear brotherhood with you, first go till you findest cross roads, there a maiden spreads out a handkerchief; if you seizest this handkerchief and bringest it here, we shall swear brotherhood with you; if you failest, you art none of us. Many have tried to take this handkerchief, but the maiden always kills them.' The devis thought that the prince would be killed too, and that they would thus get rid of him.

The prince set out and came to the cross roads, and, behold, a beautiful maiden flew down; a handkerchief was spread out in front of her, and hid her from his eyes. The prince came up and seized the handkerchief, but just as he was going away, the maiden attacked him. The prince was victorious in the fight. After the combat a golden slipper was left in the prince's hand.

He came to the devis with the handkerchief, and gave them the golden slipper, saying: 'Go to the town, change this for money, and bring it home.'

The devis sent the lame devi with the golden slipper. When he reached the town he met a merchant, to whom he showed the slipper. The merchant complained and said: 'My wife had golden slippers, you must have stolen this one.'

The devi said that they had found the slipper--he swore, but the merchant would not believe him. He took the slipper, and locked up the lame devi.

For a long time the other devis waited for their lame brother; they watched, but no lame devi was to be seen. Then they sent the ninth brother to seek him. When he arrived in the town where the devi had gone to exchange the golden slipper, he enquired after his lame brother. Hearing him ask for a lame devi, they said: 'This must be an accomplice of the thief,' and they locked him up too.

The remaining devis waited for their ninth brother, and when they saw that he did not come, the eighth was sent, but he also was taken; then the seventh, sixth, fifth, fourth, third, second, and at last the first devi went, but none of them returned.

The prince said to himself: 'What can have happened to these devis? I will go and seek them, and perchance find out what misfortune has overtaken them.' So he arose and went forth.

The merchant heard some one was again asking for the lame devi, and wished to entrap him, but the prince said: 'If I do not find the neighbour to the golden slipper, you may call us liars, and do what you wilt to the devis and me; but if I find it you hast lied, and we shall do what we wish to you.' 'Agreed!' said the merchant, and the prince went forth to seek the other golden slipper.

He travelled far, and came at last to a kingdom by the seashore. This kingdom was ruled by a maiden, fair as the sun. Whoever came to that kingdom to sell wheat was met by the maiden, who cast the wheat and its owner into the sea, and there was no escape.

When the prince heard of this, he said to himself: 'I shall bring wheat to this country, and see what the fair one can do.' He went for the wheat, and filled a boat with grain, seated himself in another boat, and set out for the kingdom. On nearing the shore there appeared, from no one knows where, a beautiful damsel. She stretched out her hand, and was about to sink the grain, when the prince struck the boat with his foot and upset it. Then he seized the maiden's hand and drew her towards him. She, seeing that she was outwitted, pulled with all her might, and escaped from his hands, but left her rings behind her.

Thus was the maiden defeated. After this, whoever wished to bring wheat brought it, and there was plenty in that kingdom.

The people of the country fell down and kissed the knees of the prince, saying: 'We beseech you, be our king.' But he would not, and replied: 'I am come on other business, I wish for nothing but to find a certain slipper,' and he told his tale. The slipper could not be found, so he arose and left that land.

He went on again and came into another country. Here he learnt that a beautiful maiden had killed the king's son, who was buried in a vault. Every night the maiden came there and beat him with twigs. When she did this he came back to life, they supped together, and passed the time merrily until morning, when she again beat him with twigs. Then he became a corpse, and she flew away.

When the prince heard this tale, he went to aid the unfortunate youth. He entered the tomb and waited. Behold, a lovely damsel flew down, took twigs from her pocket, and beat the king's son until he came back to life; they supped and made merry until morning. As she was about to beat the youth and kill him again, the prince snatched the twigs from her hand; so the king's son lived. Then the prince took him away, and led him to his father.

Here, too, the prince was offered the throne, but he did not wish to be king. 'If I could find a certain golden slipper, I should be happy,' said he; 'I must go forth and seek it.' And he set forth on his quest again.

When he had gone some way, he came to a wide plain. He presently saw a beautiful house, and said to himself: 'I wonder who lives there,' and he went on towards the house. On the way he saw an Arab feeding some mules, and said: 'Can you tell me whose house that is, brother?' The Arab looked round about and replied: 'Shall I swallow you head first or feet first?' 'I asked you about the house, why wilt you not answer?' said the prince. Again the Arab stared round and said: 'Shall I swallow you by the head or by the feet?' 'As to the matter of swallowing, I shall soon show you what I shall do,' said the prince, giving the Arab such a blow that it sent him over nine mountains. Then he struck the mules, and went to the house.

He wandered all round it, and was much delighted with its appearance. Then he went inside through a window, and visited every room. In one of these he saw a golden throne, and on it were golden slippers like the one he sought. He said to himself: 'Perhaps this is the house of the fair damsel who gave me the slipper. I shall wait and see what happens.' He sat under the throne and waited.

Soon after, there flew in a beautiful maiden, then another, yet a third, and at last the Arab. They sat down to eat. In the twinkling of an eye the Arab laid the cloth for the sisters, and whatever heart or soul could wish was spread upon it.

After a short time the eldest sister took wine and said: 'May God grant long life to the youth who took from me the handkerchief and the golden slipper.' She drank, and put the bowl down.

Then the second sister took it and said: 'Long life to the youth who snatched the rings from my hand, and gave wheat to a kingdom.' She drank, and put the bowl down. Then the youngest sister took it and said: 'Long life to the youth who took the twigs from my hand, and restored life to a prince.' She drank, and put the bowl down.

At last the Arab took the wine and said: 'Long life to the youth who gave me a blow, and sent me over nine mountains.' He drank, and put the bowl down.

Then the prince appeared from under the throne, took the wine and said: 'I have also toasts to propose. May God grant long life to the maiden from whom I took the handker-chief.' He took from his pocket the handkerchief and gave it to the eldest sister. 'May God grant long life to the maiden from whom I took the rings,' and he gave the rings to the second sister. 'May God grant long life to the maiden from whom I took the twigs.' He returned the twigs to the youngest sister, and turning to the Arab, he said: 'May God grant long life to the Arab whom I struck and sent over nine mountains.' He drank, and put down the bowl.

Then the three sisters jumped up and said: 'He will mar-ry me.' 'No! me.' And they began to quarrel. The prince said: 'Why quarrel one with another? I shall wed the youngest sis-ter, since I am the youngest of three brothers, and you elder shall wed my elder brothers.' The maidens asked him: 'What is the object of your journey here?' 'To seek for the other gold-en slipper, and lo! I have found it here,' answered the prince. 'Because of this slipper, nine brothers, devis, are imprisoned in a certain town, and if I return without it, I, too, shall be imprisoned to-day with them.' 'This slipper is yours, and as many more as you wish, take them with you, seat youself on the Arab's back, and in three hours you will be in the town,' said the sisters.

The prince did as they told him. He filled a bag with golden slippers, sat on the Arab's back, and in three hours he was in the town.

The devis rejoiced greatly. They called the merchant, and he brought slippers. He took one by one his own slippers, but, behold, not one of them would fit the golden slipper. Then, when the prince produced his bagful of golden slippers, the merchant was proved a liar.

The prince gave the merchant into the hands of the devis, and said: 'Do to him what ye please, sell all his possessions, but I must go at once on my way.' When the devis heard this, they begged him to stay with them. But he would not consent.

The prince came to the three beautiful sisters, and married the youngest. The sisters gave the Arab a saddle bag in which was everything for the journey, placed in his hand a tree, and said: 'Go to the kingdom of the prince's father, and when you are near the palace, in such and such a place, plant this tree. It will turn into a great plane tree, and underneath, a beautiful stream will flow; there, on the banks of the stream, lay the cloth, and prepare everything for our coming.'

The Arab did everything as he was commanded. Then the maidens came. Every man and woman in the kingdom heard of this, and went out to look at them. The parents were mourning for their long-lost son.

The cup of water had not changed to blood, but they had given up all hope of finding him. At last they could stand it no longer, and they too went to see the maidens.

When the prince saw his mother and father approach, he feigned surprise, and asked why they mourned. They

answered that they had lost a son, and therefore they mourned. The prince said: 'I am your long-lost son.' The king and
queen rejoiced, and took him home. They prepared such a
wedding that the roof of the palace resounded with merri-
ment.

CONKIAJGHARUNA

There was and there was not, there was a miserable peasant. He had a wife and a little daughter. So poor was this peasant that his daughter was called Conkiajgharuna[3].

Some time passed, and his wife died. He was unhappy before, but now a greater misfortune had befallen him. He grieved and grieved, and at last he said to himself: 'I will go and take another wife; she will mind the house, and tend my orphan child.' So he arose and took a second wife, but this wife brought with her a daughter of her own. When this woman came into her husband's house and saw his child, she was angry in heart.

She treated Conkiajgharuna badly. She petted her own daughter, but scolded her stepdaughter, and tried to get rid of her. Every day she gave her a piece of badly-cooked bread, and sent her out to watch the cow, saying: 'Here is a loaf; eat of it, give to every wayfarer, and bring the loaf home whole.' The girl went, and felt very miserable.

Once she was sitting sadly in the field, and began to weep bitterly. The cow listened, and then opened its mouth, and said: 'Why are you weeping? What troubles you?' The girl told her sad tale. The cow said: 'In one of my horns is honey, and in the other is butter, which you can take if you will, so why be unhappy?' The girl took the butter and the honey, and in a short time she grew plump. When the stepmother noticed this she did not know what to do for rage. She rose, and after that every day she gave her a basket of wool with her; this wool was to be spun and brought home in the evening finished. The

---

3 Conkiajgharuna is the Georgian 'Cinderella.' Conkiajgharuna refers here to the little girl in rags.

stepmother wished to tire the girl out with toil, so that she should grow thin and ugly.

Once when Conkiajgharuna was tending the cow, it ran away on to a roof.[4] The girl pursued it, and wished to drive it back to the road, but she dropped her spindle on the roof. Looking inside she saw an old woman seated, and said to her: 'Good mother, will you give me my spindle?' The old dame replied: 'I am not able, my child, come and take it yourself.' This old woman was a devi.

The girl went in and was lifting up her spindle, when the old dame called out: 'Daughter, daughter, come and look at my head a moment, I am almost eaten up.'

The girl came and looked at her head. She was filled with horror; all the worms in the earth seemed to be crawling there. The little girl stroked her head and removed some, and then said: 'You have a clean head, why should I look at it?' This conduct pleased the old woman very much, and she said: 'When you go, go along such and such a road, and in a certain place you will see three springs—one white, one black, and one yellow. Pass by the white and black, and put your head in the yellow and lave it with your hands.'

The girl did this. She went on her way, and came to the three springs. She passed by the white and black, and bathed her head with her hands in the yellow fountain. When she looked up she saw that her hair was quite golden, and her hands, too, shone like gold. In the evening, when she went home, her stepmother was filled with fury. After this she sent her own daughter with the cow. Perhaps the same good fortune would visit her!

---

4 This was originally footnoted saying that "in some parts of the Caucasus the houses of the peasantry are built in the ground, and it is quite possible to walk onto a roof unwittingly."

So Conkiajgharuna stayed at home while her stepsister drove out the cow. Once more the cow ran on to the roof. The girl pursued it, and her spindle fell down. She looked in, and, seeing the devi woman, called out: 'Dog of an old woman! here! come and give me my spindle!' The old woman replied: 'I am not able, child, come and take it yourself.' When the girl came near, the old woman said: 'Come, child, and look at my head.' The girl came and looked at her head, and cried out: 'Ugh! What a horrid head you have! You are a disgusting old woman!' The old woman said: 'I thank you, my child; when you go on your way you will see a yellow, a white, and a black spring. Pass by the yellow and the white springs, and lave your head with your hands in the black one.'

The girl did this. She passed by the yellow and white springs, and bathed her head in the black one. When she looked at herself she was black as a negro, and on her head there was a horn. She cut it off again and again, but it grew larger and larger.

She went home and complained to her mother, who was almost frenzied, but there was no help for it. Her mother said to herself: 'This is all the cow's fault, so it shall be killed.'

This cow knew the future. When it learned that it was to be killed, it went to Conkiajgharuna and said: 'When I am dead, gather my bones together and bury them in the earth. When you are in trouble come to my grave, and cry aloud: "Bring my steed and my royal robes!"' Conkiajgharuna did exactly as the cow had told her. When it was dead she took its bones and buried them in the earth.

After this, some time passed. One holiday the stepmother took her daughter, and they went to church. She placed a trough in front of Conkiajgharuna, spread 80 pounds of millet in the courtyard, and said: 'Before we come home from church fill this trough with tears, and gather up this millet, so that not one grain is left.' Then they went to church.

Conkiajgharuna sat down and began to weep. While she was crying a neighbor came in and said: 'Why are you in tears? What is the matter?' The little girl told her tale. The woman brought all the brood-hens and chickens, and they picked up every grain of millet, then she put a lump of salt in the trough and poured water over it. 'There, child,' said she, 'these are your tears! Now go and enjoy yourself.'

Conkiajgharuna then thought of the cow. She went to its grave and called out: 'Bring me my steed and my royal robes!' There appeared at once a horse and beautiful clothes. Conkiajgharuna put on the garments, mounted the horse, and went to the church.

There all the folk began to stare at her. They were amazed at her grandeur. Her stepsister whispered to her mother when she saw her: 'This girl is very much like our Conkiajgharuna!' Her mother smiled scornfully and said: 'Who would give that sun-darkener such robes?'

Conkiajgharuna left the church before any one else; she changed her clothes in time to appear before her stepmother in rags. On the way home, as she was leaping over a stream, in her haste she let her slipper fall in.

A long time passed. Once when the king's horses were drinking water in this stream, they saw the shining slipper, and were so afraid that they would drink no more water. The king was told that there was something shining in the stream, and that the horses were afraid.

The king commanded his divers to find out what it was. They found the golden slipper, and presented it to the king.

When he saw it he commanded his viziers, saying: 'Go and seek the owner of this slipper, for I will wed none but her.' His viziers sought the maiden, but they could find no one whom the slipper would fit.

Conkiajgharuna's stepmother heard this, adorned her daughter, and placed her on a throne. Then she went and told the king that she had a daughter whose foot he might look at, it was exactly the model for the shoe. She put Conkiajgharuna in a corner, with a big basket over her. When the king came into the house he sat down on the basket, in order to try on the slipper.

Conkiajgharuna took a needle and pricked the king from under the basket. He jumped up, stinging with pain, and asked the stepmother what she had under the basket. The stepmother replied: ''Tis only a turkey I have there.' The king sat down on the basket again, and Conkiajgharuna again stuck the needle into him. The king jumped up, and cried out: 'Lift the basket, I will see underneath!' The stepmother entreated him, saying: 'Do not blame me, your majesty, it is only a turkey, and it will run away.'

But the king would not listen to her entreaties. He lifted the basket up, and Conkiajgharuna came forth, and said: 'This slipper is mine, and fits me well.' She sat down, and the king found that it was indeed a perfect fit. Conkiajgharuna became the king's wife, and her shameless stepmother was left with a dry throat.

ASPHURTZELA

Once upon a time, there was once a woman. This woman's husband had died young, and left her four little children: three boys and one girl.

When the children were grown up, their mother said: 'Children, why do you not look after your patrimony? Why do you leave it thus abandoned?' The children did not know anything about this patrimony, and asked their mother where it was. The mother told them that it was in such and such a place, but the children would have to go a long way. They asked their mother: 'Since it is so far, when we go to work, who will bring us our food and drink?' The mother answered: 'I shall send your sister with your food.'

The brothers were pleased with their mother's proposal, and made ready to start. Their mother gave them onion and garlic with them, and said: 'As you are going along, cut the skin off and drop it: when your sister brings your food she will see it, and know where to find you.'

The brothers went to work, and on the path they threw down the skins as their mother had suggested.

Near this path there lived a devi with a hundred heads. Once the devi's mother saw the onion peelings strewed on the path; she collected them all, and put them on the road leading to her house. Three days passed, and the mother thought that her sons' food must be nearly finished. She prepared some more for them, put it in a bag, gave it to her daughter, and sent her to her brothers. The girl set out and followed the onion peelings.

She went on and on and came to a house. In the house was seated an old woman. The girl cried out: 'Mother, mother, can you tell me if my brothers are working here?' 'What do you want with your brothers here?' said the old woman. 'This is the house of a devi with a hundred heads; he will soon be coming home, so I had better hide you, for if he sees you he will eat you.'

The devi's mother took the maiden and hid her. The devi appeared, no one knows from where. He carried dead game and firewood. He unbound them from his back, went in, and said: 'Mother, I smell a man! Who has come here?' 'Why do you ask?' said the old woman; 'for fear that your bird cannot fly in heaven, nor can worm creep on earth.' The devi insisted, and his mother at last gave way, and said: 'I have here a maiden whom I wish you to marry; if you will not eat her, I will let you see her.' The son promised, and his mother brought the girl out. When the devi saw her, he liked her very much, and did not eat her.

The brothers waited and waited for their sister, and when she did not come they rose and went home. They reproached their mother, saying: 'Why have you not sent us food?' When their mother heard them say this, she began to weep, and said: 'Near the road dwells a hundred-headed devi, and I fear that he—may he be cursed!—has eaten her.' The brothers did not know of this devi, and when they heard about him they arose and went forth to deliver their sister.

When they had gone a good way, they neared the house of the devi. At that time their sister and the devi's mother were sitting on the roof. The devi's mother saw them coming in the distance, and said to her daughter-in-law: 'Look there! do you see nothing coming?' Her daughter-in-law replied: 'I see something like a swarm of flies.' 'Woe to their mother and to my son's mother!' said the devi's mother, and asked her again, in a short time, what she saw. The devi's wife answered: 'I see three men.' 'Woe to their mother and to my son's mother!' moaned the old woman.

The three brothers came at last to the devi's house. There they saw water, but they could not cross it by any means. They threw in stones, and stepped over in this way. Then the girl saw that they were her brothers; she came down and embraced them. When the devi's mother learnt who they were, she took them in, gave them food, and then hid them, saying: 'If my son comes home and sees you he will eat you.'

Then the hundred-headed devi came, no one knows whence. On one shoulder he had firewood, and on the other dead game. At the door he undid his burden, and, when he came in, said: 'I smell a man; who has come here?' His mother tried to hide the truth, but her son would not leave her alone, so at last she said: 'If you will promise not to eat your wife's brothers, I will show them to you.' The devi promised, and the old woman brought in the three brothers.

A little while after, the devi said to his wife's brothers: 'Come, let us prepare supper.' They all came and began to skin the game the devi had brought. While the three brothers skinned one stag, the devi skinned sixty, cut them up and threw them into the pot. Then he came, seized the stag his brothers-in-law were skinning, and threw it also into the pot.

When they sat down to supper, the devi asked his wife's brothers: 'Are you eaters of bone or eaters of flesh?' They answered: 'What have we to do with flesh? Bones are good enough for us.' The devi filled his mouth, tore off the flesh, and threw the bones to the three brothers. Then he again inquired: 'Will you drink out of a doki[5] or out of a qantsi[6]?' 'From a

---

5 A doki is an Imeretian measure of wine that holds 5 bottles.
6 A qantsi is a drinking horn.

qantsi,' replied the brothers. The devi poured out a doki of wine for himself, while he filled the qantsi for them.

When they had finished supper, and were preparing to go to bed, the devi again inquired: 'Do you wish to sleep in a bed or in the stable?' 'What have we to do with a bed? Put us in the stable!' replied the brothers. The devi lay down in his bed, and the brothers slept in the stable. In the morning, when the devi awoke, he said to his mother: 'Mother, I am hungry!' The mother saw his meaning, and not wishing to let her daughter-in-law understand, she thus replied: 'Go, son, to the stable; there, in the breadbox, are three badly-cooked loaves. Take them and eat them.'

The devi went into the stable where the brothers lay. He swallowed one of them in the doorway, put the other two in his pocket, and went into the wood.

In the meantime the mother of the brothers waited and waited, and when they did not come back, she thought: 'The devi must have eaten my sons.' She wept bitterly, her tears flowed until they reached to heaven. At that moment a man was passing by. He asked the cause of the tears, and the woman told him that they were for the loss of her children.

Then the man gave her an apple, and said: 'Cut this apple into a hundred pieces, and every day eat three; when the apple is finished, you shall have a son, and you shall call his name Asphurtzela[7].'

The woman did as he said. She cut the apple into a hundred pieces, and every day ate three. When the apple was finished, she brought forth a son, and called him by the name of Asphurtzela. Asphurtzela grew as much in a day as other children grow in a year.

---

7 Asphurtzela means a hundred leaves; the name refers to the manner of his birth.

Once when Asphurtzela was playing with a group of little boys, a woman passed by with a coca[8] full of water on her shoulder. Just then Asphurtzela threw his codchi[9]; the codchi whirled through the air, struck the woman's coca and broke it. The woman was angry, and called out: 'May you be cursed! But how can I curse you, only son of you mother? For this trick may your brothers and sister never be delivered from the claws of the devi!'

Asphurtzela did not understand this. He hastened inside, and said to his mother: 'Give me to suck, mother!' 'What a time to ask such a thing,' said his mother. But the boy would not wait, so his mother gave him his wish.

Asphurtzela bit his mother's breast, and said: 'Tell me, mother, have I any brothers?' His mother did not wish him to know, but she was in such pain that she told him everything. When Asphurtzela heard her tale, he prepared to go away. His mother entreated him not to leave her, but the boy would not be persuaded, and set out.

He wandered far and near, and came to an open field, where he saw men ploughing the ground. He shouted out to them: 'Take care, save yourselves, a hundred-headed devi is coming!' The men were filled with terror, and fled in all directions.

Asphurtzela slung the plough over his back, took it to a smith, and said: 'Make me out of this iron a pair of shoes and a bow and arrow.' The smith did so; Asphurtzela put on the iron shoes, took the bow and arrow, and went in quest of the hundred-headed devi.

He went some distance and approached the devi's house. At that time the devi's mother was sitting on the roof, and,

---

8 A coca is a large measure for fluid, containing about 25 bottles.
9 Codchi are knucklebones.

seeing some one coming, she said to her daughter-in-law: 'Do you see any one, or do my eyes deceive me?' When her daughter-in-law assured her that it was some one, the devi's mother moaned: 'Woe to his mother's breast, and woe to my son's mother's breast!'

In the meantime Asphurtzela arrived quite near the house, leaped over the stream, and came to the door. He saw there a young girl, and said: 'Surely you are my sister!' The girl only knew her three brothers, and would not admit this, but when Asphurtzela told her his tale, she believed him.

Then the devi's mother came and said: 'Come, child, I will put you in safety and hide you, lest my son eat you when he comes home.' 'Go in there, dog of an old woman! May God bring you and you son to shame!' said Asphurtzela, and he waited impatiently for the return of the devi.

Just then the devi appeared, with game slung over his shoulder, and tree roots thrust under his arm. When he saw a strange boy standing boldly in front of his house, he said to himself: 'For fear of me bird dare not fly in heaven nor worm creep on earth. Who can this boy be who is strutting about so carelessly?'

The devi was mad with fury when he saw him. Flames shot from his eyes; he cast an angry glance at him, and shouted out: 'Who art thou? and what art you doing here?' 'Shall I tell you who I am? I am you wife's brother; I am come to be you guest, so you must be my host,' said Asphurtzela. 'Very well,' returned the devi, 'come in and let us prepare supper. We must skin the game and cook it.' They began to skin the game, but by the time the devi had skinned one beast, Asphurtzela had finished all the game, thrown it into the pot and cooked it.

The devi gazed on Asphurtzela in unfeigned astonishment. When the food was cooked, and they sat down to supper, the devi, according to his custom, put the question to his guest: 'Are you an eater of bones or of flesh?' 'Pass me over the flesh, why should I eat bones? Am I a dog that I should do this?' answered Asphurtzela. The devi gave him flesh, and inquired: 'Will you drink out of a qantsi or out of a doki?' 'Pass over the doki, why should I take a qantsi?' The devi gave him the doki, and sank into deep thought. When it was time to go to bed, the devi inquired: 'Will you sleep in the stable or in a bed?' 'I am a man, what should I do in the stable? Give me a bed,' said Asphurtzela.

So it came to pass that Asphurtzela slept in the bed, and the devi lay down in the stable. He lay down, but, alas! He could not sleep. His one idea was how he could rid himself of this disagreeable guest. When he thought that Asphurtzela must be asleep, he took a huge sword and began to sharpen it. The noise of the sharpening awoke Asphurtzela, and he, guessing the devi's design, jumped out of bed, and put a log of wood under the coverlet. Then he hid in the room. When the devi had made his sword as bright as a diamond, he stole out quietly, opened the door, and went noiselessly towards Asphurtzela's bed. He raised his sword with all his might and main, and struck with such force that all the dust in the bed was raised, and the log was cleft through the middle. Then the devi went away and closed the door.

Asphurtzela shook down his bed and slept peacefully. In the morning, when the devi awoke and saw his brother-in-law, he gazed on him in amazement, and said: 'Did you feel any pain in the night?' 'Oh, no!' said Asphurtzela. 'Not even a flea-bite?' 'No.' 'Then let us wrestle.' 'Very well,' said

Asphurtzela, and the combat began.

The devi struggled and struggled, but could not move his brother-in-law. Then Asphurtzela attacked him, and buried him in the ground up to the neck. He took his bow and arrow, aimed at the devi, and cried out: 'Tell me quickly what you have done with my brothers, or I shall shoot you.' The devi was afraid, and said: 'Do not kill me and I shall tell you. In my breast is a little coffer, in it they are lying dead; there too is a handkerchief, place it on them, and they will become alive again.'

When Asphurtzela heard this, he cut open the devi's breast, took out the coffer, brought out his brothers, placed a handkerchief on them, and they came back to life. Then he shot his arrow at the hundred-headed devi and killed him. When he had cut him into small pieces, he went to the devi's mother and killed her too. Then he learnt his brothers' story, and told them his in return.

The brothers believed Asphurtzela, but envy entered their hearts when they found how much braver he was than they. At last they all arose and went towards home. On the way they had to pass through an open field, where there grew a tree, so large that the entire field was under its shade. Asphurtzela said to his brothers and sister: 'Let us rest here, I am very tired and would close my eyes a little.' The brothers consented.

Asphurtzela lay down at the foot of the tree and slept like the dead. His brothers sat down near him, and began to whisper one to another: 'Now that he has killed the hundred-headed devi, what good can he do us? Come, let us bind him to this tree and leave him here.' They took ropes, twisted them round and round, and bound him to the tree, so hard that blood poured from his fingers. When his sister saw this, she entreated them to spare him, but they would not listen to her. They bound him tight, took their sister and went home.

As soon as they were in the house, the girl told their mother everything. The mother called down curses on her three sons.

When Asphurtzela woke and saw that he was bound to the tree, he tried hard to get away, but could not move. He looked round, and saw that his brothers were no longer there. He looked everywhere, and then prayed to God: 'O God, if I have deceived my brothers, may this tree become stronger, but if they have deceived me, may I pull it up by the roots.' When he had said this he tried again, and the tree came up by the roots.

Then Asphurtzela arose and went home, bearing the tree with him. He came to the house, and called to his brothers: 'Come out at once and loose my hands!' His brothers grew pale and faint from fear, but they came out and set him free. After this Asphurtzela did not wish to live with his brothers, and made ready to leave home. His sister and mother entreated him to stay, but Asphurtzela would not yield.

He went away, and wandered on until he came to a field where a man was plowing; when he turned up a chunk of dirt he threw it into his mouth and swallowed it. Asphurtzela gazed and gazed, and at last said: 'Man, why do you swallow these chunks of dirt?' 'There is no cause for surprise in that; Asphurtzela has killed the hundred-headed devi, what is there remarkable in my swallowing clods?' said the clod-swallower. 'I am Asphurtzela, so let us be as brothers,' said Asphurtzela. They went on together.

When they had gone some distance they came to another field, where there was a man with mill wheels tied to his feet, and in his pocket were two hares. He let both the hares away, and then caught both again. Asphurtzela gazed and gazed at the man, and then said: 'Man, what art you doing? How can you catch these hares?' 'Asphurtzela killed the hundred-headed devi, what is there remarkable in catching two hares?' said the hare-catcher. 'Why, this is Asphurtzela, and he will be as a brother to you, if you will,' said the clod-swallower. So they all went on together.

On the way, the comrades arranged that each should shoot his arrow in turn, and in the place where it stuck they should eat their repast. First of all the earth-swallower shot. His arrow stuck in a very awkward place, but they came and took their supper there.

Then the hare-catcher shot his arrow, which also stuck in an awkward place. They came to it and ate their mid-day meal.

Last of all Asphurtzela cast his arrow, and it stuck on the shelf of a house where dwelt three devis. At that time the devis were being married to three fair maidens. They saw the arrow stick in their shelf, and stopped the weddings. They tried to pull the arrow out, they struggled and struggled, but could not move it. Then they said: 'Since we cannot pull this arrow out, let us go away, in case he who shot it comes and takes up his abode here.' They left in the house only one lame devi, whom they hid in the chimney.

The three friends came in, laid the cloth, and made ready their supper. They threw up their caps for joy. Then they said: 'Come, let each of us, in turn, remain at home and prepare the food.'

The first day the earth-swallower stayed in. He had prepared the food and dressed it, when, behold! the lame devi came down from the chimney, and said to the earth-swallower: 'Give me to eat and drink.' He gave him food. 'Give me to eat and drink,' said the devi again. He gave him food once more. When he made the same demand a third time, the clod-swallower answered: 'If you eat and drink everything, what shall I say to my comrades?' The devi said: 'Give me to eat and drink, or I shall eat your and your provisions too.' The clod-swallower was afraid, and ran to the door. The devi sat down and finished all the food.

The companions came home and saw that there was no food, but what did it matter? They managed for that day, and the next morning left the hare-catcher at home. The same thing happened to him as to the clod-swallower. Then it was Asphurtzela's turn.

He prepared a quantity of different kinds of food and drink for his companions. Then the lame devi came out of the chimney, and said: 'Give me to eat and drink.' Asphurtzela did so. 'Give me to eat and drink,' again said the devi. Asphurtzela did so. When he asked a third time, Asphurtzela said: 'If I give you all, what will my comrades do?' 'If you wilt not give me to eat, I shall eat your and your food too.' Asphurtzela smiled to himself, took his bow and arrow, shot the devi through the heart, and cut him in halves.

The devi's head rolled one way and his body another. The head cried out: 'Happy is he who will follow me.' The body cried: 'Woe to the man who follows me.' In the meantime Asphurtzela's companions returned. They ate, and then said:

'Let us go and see what the devi's head promised.'

The devi's head rolled and fell into a hole. Asphurtzela looked in and saw three lovely maidens. He was pleased, and said: 'Let us bring them out and marry them.' The earth-swallower slipped in, but before he had reached the bottom he called out: 'I burn, I burn, draw me up,' and they took him out. Then the hare-catcher slipped down, and the same thing happened to him. Then came Asphurtzela's turn.

He said to his companions: 'When I call out "I burn, I burn," let me down lower into the hole.' He called out many times: 'I burn,' but his companions only lowered him farther.

He went down the hole and saw the maidens, each excelled the other, but the youngest was certainly the most beautiful of all. He took the eldest, and called out to the clod-swallower: 'This is yours!' Then he sent up the second sister, calling out to the hare-catcher: 'This is yours!' Last of all he was about to send the youngest, as his wife, but she objected, saying: 'Go you first, then I will come, for I fear that you comrades will betray you.' Asphurtzela was obstinate, and insisted upon her going first. 'Very well,' said the maiden, 'I will go, since you wish me to do so, but know this, you companions will not draw you up, they will shut down the covering of the hole, and you will be left here. Three streams will flow here; one black, one blue, and one white; do not put your head under any except white water, lest you be drowned.'

It was as she had said. When all three maidens were up, the two men put stones at the mouth of the hole, and left Asphurtzela. He was so indignant that he at once put his head under the black spring, and was immediately carried to the lower regions. He wandered about here and there, and came at last to an old woman's hut. He called out: 'Mother, mother, give me some water to drink.' 'Ah, child,' said the old woman, 'at present there is none, we shall have it again when the dragon has carried away our princess.' 'What dragon?' said Asphurtzela. The old woman replied: 'Our water is withheld by a dragon, and if we do not offer him a human victim to eat, the water will not flow. We have all paid this debt save the king, and today his daughter is to be offered up.' 'Fetch me a water-vessel, mother, I must hasten this minute to the well,' said Asphurtzela.

The woman prayed him not to go, but he would not hear her. The old woman arose, and brought him vessels. Asphurtzela broke up these small water-jars, and said: 'Have you no kvevris[10]? bring them to me.' The old woman showed him where the kvevris were. Asphurtzela took them and went away.

When he came to the edge of the stream, he saw a richly dressed maiden seated, shedding bitter tears. He asked her the cause, and when he learnt that this was the king's daughter, he said: 'I will sleep here; when the dragon comes, wake me up.' He laid his head on the maiden's lap, and fell asleep. The dragon soon appeared. The maiden was afraid to wake Asphurtzela, and she wept more than ever. One of her tears fell on Asphurtzela's cheek, and he woke. When he saw the dragon he rose up, shot an arrow, and cut it in pieces. The maiden, overjoyed, immediately hastened home to her father, and said: 'Thus and thus has it come to pass, the dragon is dead.' The king at first would not believe this, but when others put faith in the story, he sent to seek the youth. He wished

---

10 Originally footnoted as "a kvevri is a large wine-jar which is kept buried in the earth up to the neck."

him to marry the princess, and decided to give him half of the kingdom.

They sought, and sought, but could not find him. Then the old woman came to the palace and said: 'Mighty sovereign! have mercy upon me and upon my son.' The king knew that she had no son, and said: 'You formerly had no son, where have you found this one?' 'God has given me for my son a youth who has killed our enemy the dragon,' answered the old woman.

The king was happy that the youth was found. He sent his ministers to bring him to the palace. When Asphurtzela came, the king offered him great presents, but he would not take them, and said: 'If you will send me back to my own land of light, I shall be happy, this is all I desire.' The king was very melancholy, he entreated him, but it was of no avail, so he promised.

After this, Asphurtzela went again to his adopted mother. On the way he saw a great tree, and on the top there was a griffin's nest. There flew down from on high a dragon, and the little birds set up a terrified scream. When Asphurtzela saw what was about to happen, he drew his bow, and, in the twinkling of an eye, the dragon was dead.

The mother griffin flew down, and her fledglings told her what had happened. Then the grateful griffin came to Asphurtzela and said: 'Tell me what you wish, that I may do you a service.' Asphurtzela said: 'I wish for nothing, except to be taken again into the land of light.' 'It will be difficult for me, but why should I not do this for your sake?' said the griffin, and directed him to get food and prepare for the journey. Asphurtzela returned to the king, and asked him for provisions.

When everything was ready, the griffin put Asphurtzela on her back and flew off. On the way, when the griffin cried out, Asphurtzela put food in her mouth. Just as they were about to enter the world of light, the griffin again cried aloud. Asphurtzela had no more food left, but he cut off the calf of his leg, and threw it into the griffin's mouth. This morsel was so very tasty that the griffin did not eat it, but kept it on the tip of her tongue.

When they had arrived, the griffin said: 'Now farewell! Leap down and go away.' Asphurtzela descended and went away, but he walked like one who is lame. The griffin said: 'What ails you that you are lame?' He told her. Then the griffin took the piece of flesh she had kept on her tongue, put it in its place, made it whole, and went away.

Asphurtzela went to seek his comrades. He went on and on until he came to a certain place. There he saw his two companions about to marry the beautiful maidens. He took aim with his bow and arrow, and called out: 'Were the men or the women to blame?' The youngest sister replied: 'How could it be the women's fault? It was the men's.' Asphurtzela shot his arrow and killed his two companions. Then he took the beautiful maidens with him, married the youngest, and gave the two elder to his brothers.

THE SHEPHERD AND THE
CHILD OF FORTUNE

Once upon a time, there was a man who had a wife. They possessed great wealth, but had no child. Once the woman said to her husband: 'Come, let us place young bulls in our churches, and at night let some one watch, perhaps God will look down upon us and give us a child.' The husband approved of this idea, and placed bulls in five churches.

Then they went into one of the churches, killed a bull, gave it to their shepherd, and said: 'Go, take this bull's flesh and give it to the poor; do you remain in the church all night and watch. Listen very carefully.' The shepherd went away and gave the bull's flesh to the poor; then he went into the church, and remained the whole night watching, but he heard not a word relating to his master's childlessness.

Day dawned, and the shepherd went and told his master: 'I have watched the whole night, and have not heard a sound.' Then this man went into the second chapel. He killed the bull there, and gave it to his shepherd, who distributed it even as he had the first. In the morning, when he went home, he brought the same answer as before. Then they went to the third and fourth chapels, but still they learnt nothing.

Only the fifth chapel remained. Here also the shepherd distributed bull's flesh to the poor, and hid himself in the church. In the middle of the night, behold there flew down the five angels of the churches, and began to talk together. They said: 'We must do something for this man. He is childless; let us give him a son.' 'Yes,' said the first angel, 'but when he reaches the age of twenty let him die and return to us.' 'No,' said the second angel, 'when the priest shall lead him into the cathedral and place a crown on his head, then he shall die.' 'When he has a wife and children, then he shall die,' said the third. 'He shall live a long time, he shall grow old, but shall be a worthless fellow,' said the fourth. 'If we are to give the man a child, let us give him something better,' said the fifth angel. 'We have spoken, now it is your turn; what do you say?' answered the others. 'Then,' said the fifth angel, 'let him be endowed with immortal youth, and whatever he asks of God may it come to pass.' 'Good, good!' assented the others, and they went away each to his own place.

The shepherd heard all this. At daybreak he came back to his master, who inquired of him: 'Well, did you hear nothing last night?' The shepherd replied: 'The five angels of the churches assembled, and they said that you shouldst have a son at the end of a year, but it is ordained that you shepherd shall be present at the birth.' 'Thank the Lord! If we have a son you may be present,' answered the husband and wife.

After this the shepherd went to his sheep, and the man and woman went in. A year passed; the shepherd delayed some time, put in his pocket a little goat, and went away. The woman was in bed, and the shepherd put her child in his pocket, and wrapped the young goat up in the bedclothes. Then the shepherd opened the bedroom door and went away. When he had gone for one or two weeks the child would not stay in his pocket any longer, and asked to be put down. The shepherd put him down, and he walked by himself.

They went on and on, and at last they became hungry. The shepherd said to himself: 'Come, I will try if the prophecy of the angels be true or not,' and he said to the boy: 'Wish that God will give us bread, that we may eat.' The boy wished, and God gave them bread. They sat down and ate, but they had no water. He wished for water, and, by their side, there murmured a beautiful spring.

The shepherd now believed in his heart that all his desires would be fulfilled, and said: 'Wish that in this plain a house completely furnished may arise, and that outside there may be a village over which I may rule, and that I may have such and such a princess for my wife.' The boy wished this, and everything was according to his desire.

Some time passed. Once the princess asked the shepherd, saying: 'How has it happened that an illustrious princess like me has married a simple shepherd?' Her husband replied: 'Heat the spit and put it on the sole of the boy's foot to see if he is asleep. If he is, then I will tell you all.' The child heard this conversation, and wished in his heart: 'O God! May my foot be hardened, so that I cannot feel anything.' The woman heated the spit, put it on the sole of the boy's foot, but he did not move. The shepherd thought that he was really asleep, and told his wife everything in detail. The child lay quiet and listened. He now learnt for the first time whose son he was, and how he had fallen into the hands of the shepherd.

Next morning at daybreak he arose and went to seek his parents. He went on and on, and everywhere asked news of his village. He came to his father's house, and said: 'Do you want a guest?' 'Truly, child, a guest is of God!' And they led him in. Then the boy asked them: 'Have you lost anything?' The master of the house replied: 'Well, child, I have lost a shepherd, and I still owe him four years' wages.' 'I saw him just now coming to you with great wealth, and with a wife and family,' said the boy.

At night, when all were asleep, the boy wished in his heart: 'O God! May the shepherd, with his house, his family, and his town, be in our courtyard to-night.'

The next morning the master of the house came to the door, and was struck with surprise. 'My God!' said he, 'how was this town built in our courtyard?' His wife said: 'What are you talking about, husband? This our courtyard, indeed! We are somewhere else.' The man replied: 'No, wife, this is our own home; that is our house, but these are certainly not the usual surroundings.' 'Well, let me look inside; if there is a boy sleeping there it must be our house.' The boy was awake, but pretended to be asleep.

The man and woman went in and saw the boy sleeping there. They awoke him and said: 'Who are you who has appeared here? We pray you to tell us what you hast done that we no longer know our own house.' The boy smiled and said: 'I told you yesterday that your shepherd was coming to you with his possessions. Behold! He came yesterday, and has taken up his abode in your courtyard. Let us call this your shepherd here.'

At that moment the shepherd awoke. When he jumped out of bed and saw the courtyard, he said to himself: 'Great art thou, O Lord! I was settled in my home, and now I am here!' He went in to his master, bent his knee, and said: 'Thus and thus have I done; I have done evil, and now I am in your hands, do to me as you will.' When the man and woman heard this tale they did not know what to do to show their joy. First one embraced the child, then the other. At length the boy said: 'I am in truth your son, but this man is also your child. He has done wrong, but you will forgive all, and give him his hire.' His father gave the shepherd his hire, and forgave him.

But still the boy was not satisfied. He said to his parents: 'This shepherd, at least, left a goat in exchange for me; if my mother brought up the goat, he brought me up. If you wish, keep the goat and I will go with him; if, however, you keep me, you ought to give him back his goat.' 'Not only will I do that, but I will also give him half of my flocks,' said the boy's father. He divided his flocks into two parts and gave one to his shepherd, and took him into his house. The boy remained with his father and mother, and they lived happily together.

THE TWO THIEVES

There was once a thief called the Big Thief. Now this Big Thief went into a town to steal. When he had gone some little distance he met an unknown man. 'God give you victory[11]! May you be victorious!'[1] said they one to another. 'Who are you, and what is your trade?' inquired the Big Thief. 'My trade is thieving, and my name is Little Thief,' said the unknown. 'I, too, am a thief, so let us join partnership.' He agreed, and they became partners.

And they went on together to steal. On the way, the Big Thief said to the Little Thief: 'Now give me a proof of your skill in thieving.' But the latter said: 'You are the Big Thief, you must show me your skill; what can I do compared with you?' The Big Thief consented.

They saw, just at that moment, a pigeon sitting on a plane tree. The Big Thief said: 'Now you shall see me pull out the tail of that pigeon on the plane tree without its knowledge.' Having said this, he went up the tree.

When he had gone about half way, the Little Thief silently stole under the plane tree, climbed up, and while the Big Thief pulled out the tail of the pigeon, the Little Thief took off his companion's drawers, and promptly descended the tree.

When the Big Thief came down and proudly showed the pigeon's tail, the Little Thief thrust his hand into his pocket and showed him the drawers. When the Big Thief saw this, he was struck with amazement, and said: 'Although I am famous I do not think you are at all inferior to me.' They had tried each other's skill, and went on.

On the way, the Little Thief enquired of the Big Thief:

---

11 This is a customary Georgian greeting.

'What shall we steal tonight?' 'Let us go tonight and break into the king's treasury,' said the Big Thief. 'Very well,' agreed his comrade, and they set out for the town.

At nightfall, when the tread of people's feet had ceased, the thieves took two bags, and went to break into the king's treasury. The Little Thief said: 'Climb you into the treasury, gather up the money, I shall fill the bags, then we can take them up, and make off.' The Big Thief would not consent. 'No,' said he; 'you are the smaller, go inside, and I shall stay here.' He insisted until he gained his point.

At last the Little Thief got in, and collected the money. The Big Thief stayed outside and filled the bags. When the two bags were full, he made a sign, the Little Thief came out of the treasury, they took the bags and went home.

Next morning the king went into his treasury. He looked in and saw what had happened. Then he called his council together, and made his complaint. They planned and planned, and at last thought of the following scheme. They took a big barrel, filled it with pitch, and placed it at the entrance to the treasury.

The thieves knew nothing of this. When night came again, they returned to steal. The Little Thief said: 'Yesterday I went into the treasury, today it is your turn, I will watch for you.' The Big Thief consented. He went into the treasury, and suddenly was caught. The Little Thief pulled hard, but his companion could not get away; nothing but his head was visible; he was up to the neck in pitch. When day dawned, the Little Thief saw that nothing could be done, so he took his dagger and cut off his comrade's head. Then he hid it in a place where no human being could possibly find a trace of it.

He went home and told his late companion's wife. He

warned her to be very careful, and not to go out, for if it was discovered that they were interested in the dead man, they would most certainly be seized and killed.

When day dawned, they told the king: 'A thief is caught in the trap, but he has no head.' The king went himself, and saw that in truth the thief had no head, and he was amazed. How could a headless man thieve? Then he commanded them, saying: 'Take his body and put it in the market place, with sentinels to guard it. Whoever passes by and weeps at the sight of it will be guilty, because it will be a sign of pity for the thief; bring such persons to me immediately.'

When the Little Thief heard this, he went home, and instructed his companion's wife how to act. 'Take good care not to go out, lest they discover you'; and he told her what orders the king had given. The Big Thief's wife could not bear this, and entreated him to let her go, saying: 'I will stand far away and weep quietly, no one will recognise me.' 'Very well, but be careful. Take a water jug with you as if to carry water, and when near your husband's body, strike your foot against a stone, break the jar, and then sit down and weep as if you are mourning for the broken pitcher.'

The woman did exactly as she was told. She took the jar on her shoulder and went for water. When she came near the place where her husband's body was lying, she struck her foot on a stone, let the jar fall, and it broke. Then she sat down by the fragments and began to weep bitterly, apparently for the pitcher, but really for her husband. When she had wailed enough she rose and went away. The sentinels were amazed: 'What a miserable woman to cry thus for a broken pitcher!'

Night came on. The sentinels returned to the palace with the body of the thief, and said to the king: 'We saw no one who wept except one woman, who struck her foot against a stone and broke her water jar, and for this she cried bitterly.' The king was very angry, for he saw the trick the woman had played. He was enraged because they had not seized her and brought her to him, but had let her escape. Then the king ordered the sentinels' heads to be cut off.

As this ruse had not succeeded, the king thought of another. He sent the thief's corpse outside the town, and left it there. Perhaps the right person will see it and come to steal it. Sentinels were posted, and told that if any one came to steal the corpse they should seize him and bring him.

On hearing this news the Little Thief drove an ass before him into a neighboring village. There he had some cakes baked and turkeys and fowls roasted, put them in the saddlebag, and hung it on the ass. Then he bought some of the best wine and went on his way. He came to the place where the sentinels were posted, and cried out: 'Do you not want a guest? I have come from afar, and must stay here to night; I fear some one may steal the ass. Let us have a good supper.' The mention of supper delighted the sentinels. They sat down and began to eat. The Little Thief poured them out wine. The sentinels drank, but the thief did not drink a drop.

When they had eaten well, he said to them: 'I am going to sleep. As I am sleepy, you may watch the ass and see that no one steals him, lest if he be lost I accuse you to the king.' 'Lie down and make yourself easy. This ass of yours is not so attractive that you need fear for him,' said the sentinels. The Little Thief lay down and pretended to go to sleep, but he kept a sharp look out. A short time afterwards the sentinels lay in a deep sleep, they slept as if they were dead.

Then the Little Thief arose and lifted the body of his late

companion on his back. He brought forward his ass, put the corpse on it, and turned its head towards home. He himself laid down again and fell asleep.

The ass was accustomed to finding his way home, he lowered his head as if meditating, went straight home and knocked against the door. The Big Thief's wife came and took down the dead body, put it on a couch and wept. When her heart was solaced by tears, she buried him in the earth under the couch.

When morning came, the sentries awoke and roused their false host. The Little Thief looked round and called his ass. He saw that it was not there, and set up a fearful howl: 'I will go and accuse you to the king.' The sentinels were terrified, and completely lost their heads when they saw that the corpse was gone. They drew money from their pockets, and offered it to silence their noisy host. This was what he wanted; he had not only stolen the body but gained some money.

The sentinels went to the king. When he heard their tale he was extremely irritated, and ordered their heads to be cut off.

This new plan having failed, he thought of another. A street was strewed with money; sentinels were placed here and there, and ordered to seize any passer-by who gathered up the money, for he would be the thief's master and companion.

The Little Thief heard this news with joy. He got a pair of boots tarred, and went out with them under his arm.

When he came to the street that was strewed with money he sat down, took off his boots, and put on the newly-tarred boots. Then he walked along the street boldly, singing a song. When he had got to the end of the street, he took off the money that had stuck to his tarred boots, made a hole in the earth and poured it in. Then he walked back to the other end of the street, cleaned his boots again and buried the money. He did this the whole day, and by the evening he had picked up almost half of the money.

The sentinels gathered up what was left, went to the king, and said: 'No one has taken the money, but a man was walking in the street from morning till night.' The king was enraged that they had not taken this man, and ordered the sentinels to be beheaded.

Then he assembled his counselors and asked their advice. Now the king had a deer, if they were to let this animal loose it would fall on its knees before the house of him who was guilty against the king. And the viziers said: 'Let the deer go, and it will fall on its knees in front of the house of the thief.'

The king took this advice, and they let the deer loose.

It raced along the streets, and fell on its knees just in front of the Little Thief's house.

In the morning, when the Little Thief awoke, he looked out of his window, and saw the king's deer kneeling in front of his house. He had heard of this deer before, so, when he saw it, he knew what it meant. He went outside, seized hold of the hind and drew it in; he killed it and skinned it, then he hid the skin carefully, and kept the flesh in the house.

The king was mad with rage when they sought his deer and could not find it. He assembled his viziers, and told the story of the lost deer. The viziers' resources were at an end now, they could think of no other trap for the thief.

But there appeared, from no one knows where, an old woman. She approached the king and said: 'What will you give me if I find the lost deer?' 'Whatever you ask for,' said the king. 'Then give me my freedom.' 'I shall not only give you your freedom, but shall raise you to the rank of princess,' replied the king. The old woman rose and went forth to seek the deer.

She wandered till at last she came to the Little Thief's house. The Little Thief was not at home, and she saw the Big Thief's wife. She said: 'Daughter, if you have a piece of deer's flesh do not grudge it to me, it will cure a sick one of his illness.' The thief's wife did not know of the cunning of the old woman, went into her house, and brought out a piece of deer's flesh. The old woman was joyful, and did not wait. She rose and went away.

When she had gone a little way, she met the Little Thief, who said: 'What is that, old dame?' 'A piece of deer's flesh, as a remedy for my trouble! The woman in that house gave it to me,' said the beldam. The Little Thief understood her; he saw through her cunning, and said: 'What is the use of this morsel of flesh? Come with me and I can give you a whole dishful. You can eat and give it to your friends; it will be of service to you.' The old woman's head swam with pleasure. She turned back and went with the Little Thief. Whenever the deceitful old woman was enticed into the house, he drew out his dagger and cut off her head. Then he took her body, and buried it also under the couch. The king waited for news, but the old woman never came.

Some time passed by, but still the old woman did not come, and the king was enraged. He assembled his counselors, and said: 'What is the use of all this? Is there no way of trapping this thief?' The viziers said: 'This fellow is so brave, and such a clever thief, that we cannot entrap him.'

Then the king rose up and said: 'Let the thief come to me.

I shall not harm him, but shall give him my daughter to wife. He is so clever that I cannot take him by trickery.'

When the Little Thief heard this he came to the king and said: 'I am that thief, and I am come to do your majesty's will.' The king could not break his word, so he gave him his daughter in marriage.

A neighboring monarch heard this story. Every day he wrote irritating letters to the thief's father-in-law, the king, saying: 'Are you not ashamed to have anything to do with a low thief, to marry him to your daughter, and call him son-in-law?' The king was very much annoyed at these scornful reproaches, and at last fell ill, being able to bear them no longer.

Then the king's son-in-law came to him and said: 'What is the matter? Why are you ill?' His father-in-law told him everything, and he replied: 'Why distress yourself? Give me a few days' leave, and I shall show you a sight. Only on such and such a day prepare a grand festival, and I shall be here.' He fixed a date, and went away.

He travelled on until he came to the kingdom of the mocking monarch, and he went into a house and rested. The next day he saw a tailor and said: 'I want a robe cut out of pieces of skin; it must be all of different colors, and I want little bells put in it.' When the tailor had finished the garment, the thief gave him money and sent him away.

Then he clad himself in the robe, took a glittering, naked sword in his hand, and went to the palace. The porters did not want to let him in, but the thief said: 'I am Michael Gabriel, sent from God! I am commanded to take the souls of your king and queen to Paradise, and if you trouble me I shall take your souls too, and shall send them into hell.' He moved towards one of them, and the bells began to ring. The porters' hearts were fearful, and they hid themselves.

The thief went in to the king. When he saw the man he became pale. Michael Gabriel said: 'I give you a term of three days. In these three days put all your affairs in order; appoint your successor. Strip off everything, put yourselves in coffins, and set the keys on the top. In three days I shall come again, lock the coffins, and take them away with me.' When he had said this he went away, returned to the house, took off the robe of skins, and waited three days.

On the third day he clothed himself as before, and went again to the palace. The king and queen had stripped off everything, and were in the coffins waiting. He called out: 'When you get to Paradise you will hear a noise, then the coffins will open, and your eyes will view a glorious scene.' He took the keys, locked both the coffins, took them on his back, and carried them out.

He put them on his ass, went behind it, and called gently, 'Giddy-up!' On the appointed day he came to the court of his father-in-law, who had invited the whole of his kingdom and many neighboring princes to a great feast. The thief came, and, as he lifted the coffins off the ass, beautiful music was heard.

The thief opened the coffins, and the king and queen jumped out naked and began to dance. The people saw their stupidity, and were ready to die with laughing. Then the king came, clothed them in royal robes, and said: 'Now you can go back to your own country, and rule your kingdom, but do not mock me any more.' After this the king loved his son-in-law very much, and, when he died, left him the kingdom.

THE FOX AND
THE KING'S SON

There was once a king who had a son. Every one treated him badly, and chased him away. Even passers-by looked upon him with disfavor. The prince thought and thought, and at last he mounted his horse, took his bow and arrow, and departed from his father's palace.

When he had gone some distance he came into a sheltered wood. He wandered about until he found a suitable nook. He built for himself a mud hut, and dwelt there.

Every day the prince went out to hunt. He would shoot a stag or a roebuck, and bring it home. After he had eaten as much as he wanted, there was always enough meat left for the next day, but he never ate it the next day, as he went hunting again, and there was thus always a quantity of food left over.

A fox perceived this, and every day, when the prince had gone out to the chase, he stole into the hut and ate all the food that was left; then he stole away again. Some time passed thus. Then the fox said: 'There is no bravery in this! I carry away all his meat secretly, yet there is plenty. I will show myself to him.'

Once when the prince was hunting, the fox stole in, and, when his hunger was satisfied, he went about arranging everything. When the prince came home, the fox leaped out in front of him. The prince drew his bow, and was just about to shoot him, when the fox cried out: 'Do not kill me, and I will help to make your fortune!' The prince did not kill him, and the fox attended to the horse, and led it about, until the sweat dried off its coat. They lived thus for some time. The fox lighted the fire, tidied the hut, and did all the work.

But, in spite of this, there was still meat left. 'I will go and find some one who will help to eat it,' said the fox. He went out, and saw a wolf hardly able to walk from want of food. It could scarcely move from the spot where it was. The fox said: 'Come home with me, and you shalt have plenty of everything.' The wolf followed him. They both went into the hut, where the fox told his companion: 'I will tidy the house, you must stay here, and when the master comes in attend to his horse.'

The master came, and on the saddle of his horse was slung a stag. The wolf sprang out to attend to the horse; the youth drew his bow, and was about to shoot the wolf, when the fox cried out: 'Do not kill him, he is a friend!' The prince did not kill him, but jumped down from his horse, took the stag, and went in. The wolf attended to the horse, and led him up and down, while the fox himself saw to the inside of the house; thus they lived for some time.

The fox noticed that there was much meat left even now. He ran out and brought in a famished bear. The wolf was sent for grass, the bear commanded to tend the horse, while the fox arranged the house. In a little time the prince came in, and when the bear jumped out to look after his horse he drew his bow to shoot him, but the fox cried out: 'Do not kill him, he is a friend!' The youth did not kill the bear, and he tended the horse and led it about; then the wolf came in with the grass, and gave it to the horse.

Some time passed. The fox saw that even yet there was meat to spare. He went out and sought until he found an eagle, which he brought home. He commanded the eagle to attend to the horse, sent the bear for grass, and the wolf for wood to burn, while he saw to household affairs. Thus each had his business to do. When the master returned, the eagle flew out to tend the horse. The prince was about to shoot him, when the fox cried out: 'Do not kill him, he is a friend!' The prince did not kill him, but thought to himself: 'What will this vile fox bring in next? I shall see all the game in the country here.' They lived thus some time.

Once the fox said to his master: 'Give us leave to go away for two weeks; at the end of that time we shall return to you.' The master gave them leave, and thought to himself: 'I do not mind if I never see you again, for I am afraid of you all.' The fox, the wolf, the bear, and the eagle went away. They saw a glade in the wood, and rested there. The fox said to his companions: 'Now, let us build a good house for our master.' They all agreed, and set to work. The wolf cut down trees, the bear cut the wood into shape, and did the joiner work, the eagle carried it, and the fox gave orders. When the wood was ready, they set to and built the house. They built so beautiful a house that the prince could not have imagined one like it, even in his dreams. Everything was finished, but there was no furniture in it.

The fox arose and took his companions into a neighboring town. They went into the bazaar, and looked at the house-furniture. Each one had his work to do again. The fox chose the goods, the wolf was ordered to break the shutters, the bear to carry the things to the door, and the eagle to take everything to the palace. They seized everything necessary for furnishing a house—domestic utensils, carpets, and vessels. They carried them to the palace, and placed them there; so now all was finished, and there was nothing more left to wish for.

Two weeks had expired, so the four went home. The prince was hunting, but they went to meet him. They surrounded him, and would not let him pass. The fox cried out: 'I command you to come with us where we lead you.' The prince was afraid, he did not know what it could mean, but went with them. In a little while they arrived in the glade. It was girded by a wall over which no bird could fly. They opened the gates and went inside. When the king's son saw, he was stupefied with surprise. Inside the wall was laid out a beautiful garden, with fountains playing, and there stood a magnificent palace. Then they said: 'We have made all this ready in two weeks, now live happily in it.' The prince rejoiced greatly, and gave hearty thanks to his fox.

Some time passed after this. The fox said: 'I must see if I can find a good wife for my master.' He came to the prince, and again asked a fortnight's absence. Then he went away and made a sledge. He harnessed the wolf and bear to it, and said to the eagle: 'Fly up high, and keep a watch; when you see a beautiful princess, seize her in your claws and carry her off.' He himself sat down and acted as coachman. Thus they travelled from place to place.

In the villages, the fox played the trumpet, and the bear and the wolf leaped and danced along. Crowds of people came out to look. When they came to the capital, a maiden, fair as the sun, looked from her window, the eagle seized her in his claws, and flew off. The bear and the wolf turned round and started for home. When the people saw this, they all set off in pursuit. The fox was behind his companions, and the dogs came nearer, and almost touched his cloak, but in some way or other they all escaped, and brought the fair one to their master.

The king's son could scarcely stand on his feet for joy. The princess's father was in the greatest consternation, and said: 'To him who finds and brings back my daughter will I give the half of my kingdom.' But none was able to find trace of her. At last an old woman appeared, and said to the king: 'I will find your daughter.' She arose and went forth. At last she came to the prince's house, and asked: 'Do ye not want an attendant? I will come for small wages.' The fox, wolf, bear, and even the beautiful princess herself, said: 'We do not want you, we shall not take you.' But the prince did not agree with them, and engaged her as servant.

The old woman served them faithfully for a long time, and did not harm them. Then one day, when the prince was asleep, the old woman wanted the princess to go out into the garden with her. She did not wish to go, but the old woman pressed her until she consented. When they came to the fountains, the old woman offered her some water. The princess refused it, but the old woman insisted. She placed a large jar full of water to her lips, and it suddenly swallowed up the princess. Then the old woman put it to her own mouth, and it swallowed her. The large jar rolled away. The fox saw and pursued, but that which he sought was soon lost to sight.

The fox reproached his master, but it was no use saying anything now. He asked again for a fortnight's leave, made another sledge like the former, and harnessed the bear and wolf to it. He sat up on the seat, and held tambourines in his paws. He struck them, and the wolf and bear pranced and danced along. The eagle flew up high, and looked round. All the people in the land came out to gaze at the sight. The king was angry with his beautiful daughter, and said, 'Do not go out! Do not even look out.' The eagle watched for a long time, but could not see her. At last he caught a glimpse of the princess through a little window; he struck against it, broke it, seized the princess, and flew away. He rejoined his companions, and all hastened off.

They brought the princess to their master. The king collected all his army, and sent the old woman with it to the prince's palace. The fox saw them appearing in the distance like a swarm of flies. He ordered the eagle to carry stones up high in the air. When the army approached, the eagle let the stones fall on the men; the fox, the bear, and the wolf attacked them, and completely exterminated them. There escaped only one single man; they fell upon him too, gnawed one of his feet, and said: 'Go and tell you king what has befallen his hosts.'

When the king saw his man, and heard the sad end of his army, he was out of his mind with grief. He assembled all of the chief priests in his kingdom, went in front of them, and they all came on bended knees. When they were near, the fox saw them, and told his master. The prince ran out to meet them, raised them all on their feet, and took them into his house. The father and son-in-law became reconciled, and lived happily together. Then the fox said to his master: 'I am getting old now, and the day of my death will soon be here, promise to bury me in a fowl-house.' The prince promised. The fox said to himself: 'Come, I will see if my master means to keep his promise,' and he stretched himself out as if he were dead. When the prince saw the corpse, he ordered it to be taken away and thrown into the earth.

The fox was enraged, jumped up and cried out: 'Is this the way you remember my goodness to you? Well, since you hast done thus, when I die you will all be cursed, and there will not remain a trace of you.' Some time after this the fox died. After his death, his word came to pass, and they were all destroyed. The wolf, the bear, and the eagle remained masters of the field.

THE KING AND THE APPLE

Once upon a time, there was a king. When the day of his death was drawing nigh, he called his son to him, and said: 'In the day when you go to hunt in the east, take this coffer, but only open it when you art in dire distress.'

The king died, and was buried in the manner he had wished. The prince fell into a state of grief, and would not go outside the door. At last the ministers of state came to the new king, and proposed to him that he should go out hunting. The king was delighted with the idea, and set out for the chase with his suite.

They went eastwards, and killed a great quantity of game. On their way home, the young monarch saw a tower near the road, and wished to know what was in it. He asked one of his viziers to go and try to find out about it. He obeyed, but first said:

'I hope to return in three days, and if I do not I shall be dead.'

Three days passed, and the vizier did not return. The king sent a second, a third, a fourth, but not one of them came back. Then he rose and went himself. When he arrived, he saw written over the door: 'Enter and you will repent; enter not and you will repent.'

'I must do one or the other,' said the king to himself, 'so I shall go in.'

He opened the door and went in. Behold! There stood twelve men with drawn swords. They took his hand and led him into twelve rooms. When he was come into the twelfth, he saw a golden couch, on which was stretched a boy of eight or nine years of age. His eyes were closed, and he did not utter a word. The king was told:

'You may ask him three questions, but if he does not understand and answer all of them, you must lose your head.'

The king became very sad, but at last remembered the coffer his father had given him. 'What greater misfortune can I have than to lose my head?' said he to himself. He took out the coffer and opened it; from it there fell out an apple, which rolled towards the couch. 'What help can this be to me?' said the king.

But the apple began to speak, and told the following tale to the boy—'A certain man was travelling with his wife and brother, when night fell, and they had no food. The woman's brother-in-law went into a neighboring village to buy bread; on the way he met brigands, who robbed him and cut off his head. When his brother did not return, the man went to look for him; he met the same fate. The next day the unhappy woman went to seek them, and there she saw her husband and brother-in-law lying in one place with their heads cut off; around was a pool of blood. The woman sat down, tore her hair, and began to weep bitterly. At that moment there jumped out a little mouse. It began to lick the blood, but the woman took a stone, threw it at the mouse, and killed it. Then the mouse's mother came out and said: "Look at me, I can bring my child back to life, but what can you do for your husband and his brother?" She pulled up an herb, applied it to the little mouse, and it was restored to life. Then they both disappeared in their hole. The woman rejoiced greatly when she saw this; she also plucked of the same herb, put the heads on the bodies, and applied it to them. Her husband and brother-in-law both came back to life, but alas! she had put the wrong heads on the bodies. Now, my sage youth! Tell me, which was the woman's husband?' concluded the apple.

He opened his eyes, and said: 'Certainly it was he who had the right head.'

The king was very glad.

'A joiner, a tailor, and a priest were travelling together at one time,' began the apple. 'Night came on when they were in a wood; they lighted a huge fire, had their supper, and then said: "Do not let us be deprived of employment, each of us shall in turn watch, and do something in his trade." The joiner's turn came first. He cut down a tree, and out of it he fashioned a man. Then he lay down, and went to sleep, while the tailor mounted guard. When he saw the wooden man, he took off his clothes and put them on it. Last of all, the priest acted as sentinel. When he saw the man he said: "I will pray to God that He may give this man a soul." He prayed, and his wish was granted.'

'Now, my boy, can you tell me who made the man?'

'He who gave him the soul.'

The king was pleased, and said to himself: 'That is two.' The apple again went on: 'There were a diviner, a physician, and a swift runner. The diviner said: "There is a certain prince who is ill with such and such a disease." The physician said: "I know a cure for it." "I will run with it," said the swift runner. The physician prepared the medicine, and the man ran with it. Now tell me who cured the king's son?' said the apple.

'He who made the medicine,' replied the boy. When he had given the three answers, the apple rolled back into the casket, and the king put it in his pocket. The boy arose, embraced the king, and kissed him: 'Many men have been here, but I have not been able to speak before: now tell me what you wish, and I will do it.' The king asked that his viziers might be restored to life, and they all went away with rich presents.

THE THREE PRECEPTS

Once upon a time, in a certain country, a certain realm, a certain region, a certain village, there was an orphan so poor, so poor, that between heaven and earth nothing could be found that was his. Being in such a plight today, tomorrow, the day after tomorrow, this week, next week, this month, next month, sad and thoughtful he became; he thought, he thought, he thought, and at last made up his mind: 'I will arise and try my luck,' he said. He rose betimes in the morning, called on the name of God, turned himself to the right hand[12], and set forth from the house.

He went, he went, he went, beyond the sky, across the earth, across the forest, across the field, across the plain, over the mountains, he went as far as he could, and when he looked he saw a man of graceful mien coming towards him. The youth quickened his step and they met. 'I wish you victory, good youth![13]' said the stranger, 'where are you going?' 'May God send you victory, my master,' answered the young man, 'I go to seek a livelihood.' 'Be my servant for three years, and I shall teach you three things that will afterwards be helpful,' said this clever man to the youth. The youth agreed, and went away with him.

At the end of a year's service, the clever man said to the youth: 'Whatever you see outside youe yard, throw it into the yard.' When the second year had passed, he again spoke to the youth, and said: 'Lend nothing to anybody unless you arw much pressed to do so.' The third year came to an end, and it

12 This was originally footnoted as "When a Mingrelian undertakes a journey, he turns to the right several times before his door and then sets out. This is held to be a favorable omen."
13 A customary salutation in Georgia.

was time for the young man to depart; the clever man called him and said: 'Tell not your secret to a woman.' Then he bade him farewell, blessed him, and sent him home. The youth set out: he went, he went, he went by day, he went by night, over land, over water, and when he reached home he began to establish himself, he made a fence round his yard and, as he had been instructed, threw into the yard all he found outside the yard.

One morning he went out and found on the road a red snake; he remembered the instruction of the clever man and threw the snake into the yard. A week later, the young man noticed that on the place where he had thrown the snake, it had laid a multitude of precious stones. It is no wonder that the youth was greatly pleased at this. He gathered up the snake and the precious stones in the skirt of his garment, and put the snake in a nest in his own house. Every day the snake laid him a precious stone. The youth became wealthy: he built himself a fine house, took a wife, and lived like a lord. Still the snake went on laying precious stones, the youth became richer and richer, and gave himself up to gladness. One day his wife said to him: 'Young man! Who has made you so fabulously rich, for you were formerly poorer than any one on earth.' 'Who? God gave me wealth,' said the husband, following the clever man's advice, not revealing his secret. But the woman gave him no peace; day and night she always asked the same thing: 'How didst you become wealthy? You must tell me, you must.' The youth had no way of escape, she wearied him out, and at last made him tell her all about the snake. Since there was nothing else to be done, the young man took his wife and showed her the snake that laid precious stones. After this, it happened that the snake ceased to lay precious stones; the young man's wealth began to diminish, and nothing was added to it.

When he was in this state, a certain man came and asked him for the loan of a knife. Of course, being utterly cast down with grief and sorrow, he remembered not the words the clever man had spoken to him, and lent the knife. May it happen to your enemy as it happened to him! It happened that this wretched man was a thief. When he had got the knife he went and broke into a house to steal; there he thrust the knife into the belly of a sleeping man, slayed him, and left the knife in the dead man's body, then pillaged the house. Afterwards an enquiry was made into the matter. They found the knife in the man who had been killed and robbed, and it turned out to be the knife of the young man. Of course he was taken and bound, all his goods were seized, and he was treated as a thief ought to be treated. Thus did it happen to the wretched youth who disobeyed the instructions of the clever man.

> *Yester eve I was there,*
> *This evening I am here...*
> *Three apples, three pomegranates,*
> *May God send you,*
> *Ripe in your hands.*
> *The tale, the tale is ended...*
> *You have eaten maize-bread with ashes[14],*
> *You have drunk bad, stale wine,*
> *And eaten a rotten walnut.*

---

14 This was originally footnoted as "Chkidi, bread made of Indian corn, is generally used in Mingrelia. It is cooked on the ashes, and the latter are often found sticking to it."

KAZHA-NDII[15]

There was once a king who had three sons and three daughters. When the day of his death was come, he called all his children, and said to his sons: 'Hearken to my will, and see that ye fulfill it. When I die, let each of you watch my tomb for one week, give these maidens to the suitors who ask for their hands.' After he had said farewell, the king died.

He was buried, and on the first night the eldest brother went to guard the grave. But in a short time something began to approach with a mighty noise, and when it came near, it was so strong that it drove the prince out of the enclosure. From a distance, the prince saw how the being that had come with noise went to the king's grave, dug up the corpse, and wept over it till morning; when morning came, it buried the corpse in the earth again, and went away. When the prince reached home, he was ashamed to say anything about what had happened.

At that time, both the elder brothers set out for the chase; the youngest brother was left at home, he heard a voice and looked round. It turned out to be a suitor for the hand of his sister. He took and gave him the eldest sister. Soon after, he again heard a voice. The prince looked round--another suitor had come. The absence of his brothers somewhat disturbed him, but, according to his father's will, he married his second sister also. A little later, a third voice was heard, and to him he gave his third sister.

In the evening, when the two elder brothers came home, they did not see their sisters; they asked the youngest, and he told them what had happened. They were not pleased, and

---

15 Ndii is the equivalent of devi in Georgian (i.e., an evil spirit).

sent him out to feed the sheep. That night the middle brother went to guard the king's grave; the same thing happened to him as to his elder brother, but he too was silent on the subject. When he reached home, the youngest brother began to entreat his elder brothers, saying: 'Be just, let me also watch my father's grave.' But they were angry, and answered: 'Get you gone, how could you guard the grave when we are not able to do it!' But afterwards they said one to the other: 'Let us allow him to go.'

So the youth went, came to the tomb of his father, lighted a candle, and, as soon as he sat down, an uproar began, but he was not affrighted. At the approach of the monster an earthquake began, but the youth was not afraid, he swung his sword round his head, and cleft the monster in twain, but the monster's blood put out the candle. Looking round, the youth saw, some way off, the blaze of a fire. He arose and went there. On his way he said to the cock: 'Crow not, so that dawn break not till I come back again, or I shall slay you.' When he came near, he met with a vast river like a sea. When he had swum over and reached the other side, the youth saw that the fire was burning among the demis[16], who were sitting round it—so he stopped and bethought himself seriously; but, at last, he took a leap, jumped into the middle of them, seized a burning brand, and ran away.

The burning cinders and ashes were showered over the demis, but they did not see the youth. The youth went back, but as he crossed the river the burning log went out. He was angry at this, but what could he do? He went back again, and when he threw himself upon the fire the demis caught him, and asked what he wanted. He told them. The demis said to

---

16 Demis are the equivalent of devis and ndiis in Georgian.

him: 'In that castle there dwelled three maidens unseen by the sun[17], you must bring them to us or we will not let you go.' The youth asked them: 'Is there a ladder up to the castle?' They answered: 'Yes.' 'Then let us go,' said he.

He took all the demis with him, and said: 'I shall climb up first, then you must come one by one.' They agreed. The youth went up, one demi came after him. As soon as the first demi reached the top, the youth brandished his sword, slayed him, and laid down his body. When the second came up, he did likewise unto him. Thus he slayed them all, one by one, and left their bodies there.

Then he went in, saluted the maidens, and gave each of them a ring--to the youngest for himself, to the others for his brothers. The youth went out, thrust his sword into a stone, and left it there, took fire with him, and went back. When he had crossed the river, he cried to the cock: 'Now crow!' Then he went to his father's grave. Till dawn he stayed there, and then he went home.

The beautiful maidens told the king what had happened. The king ordered all his subjects to be summoned, and asked: 'Who is able to draw this sword out of the stone?' But nobody could draw it out. Then the king made a proclamation: 'To him that can draw out this sword I will give my daughter.' The princes, as soon as they heard of this, decided to go there. When they were making ready for the journey, the youngest asked his brothers to take him too. At last they consented to take him. When they arrived, they found a great uproar:

---

17 "This phrase is continually applied to beautiful girls in Georgian poetry. It has three meanings: (1) A girl strictly kept, and not seen out of doors; (2) One who is not sunburnt, fair complexioned; (3) A maiden such as the sun has never seen the like of for beauty. The last meaning is the most frequent."

people from all parts of the world were, in turn, laying hold of the sword, but could not draw it out. Last of all, the youngest brother came up, pulled out his sword, put it in the scabbard, and said to the king: 'All three daughters are ours now, for I have two brothers.' He called his brothers, and they took the three maidens to wife. Great merry-making began.

The king gave to the wife of the youngest prince a flying carpet, which carried away any one who sat on it. The princess sat on it, and followed her suite. The groomsmen and youths set out with them. When they had gone half way, a monster swooped down on the princess and carried her off. A sad uproar began, but what was to be done? The young prince said to his brothers: 'Farewell! I must perish with her,' and went away.

He went, he went, he went, he went as far as he could, and in a field he found a spring, beside which he lay down. There came a boy with a water jug. The prince asked: 'Whose village is this?' The boy replied: 'Here dwell three brother demis, all married to daughters of one king.'

When the youth heard this he was glad, for it turned out that his sisters dwelt here. When he came near, the sisters went out to meet him. It is easy to imagine how glad they were to see him. When it was dark, the three demis returned. One of the sisters went out to meet them, and said: 'My brother is come.' The demis answered: 'If the elder brothers come, we can make roast meat of them, if it be the youngest, we shall know how to do him honor.' The demis went in, and kissed the youth for joy at meeting him.

As they were all sitting round the hearth, the demis began to sigh deeply. The youth asked them: 'Why do you sigh?' 'Why? We are sorry for that poor damsel! Kazha-

Ndii-Kerkun[18] was carrying through the air a golden-haired woman; we pursued, but only succeeded in pulling off a lock of the woman's hair.' They showed the hair to the youth. As soon as he saw it he fainted, crying: 'Ah! Woe is me! Woe is me!' The demis asked him what was wrong. He told them all. As soon as day dawned, the youth arose, and made ready to depart. The demis were very sorry at this, but what could they do? They gave him a horse and a little dog.

The youth set out, and came to the house of Kazha-Ndii; but Kazha-Ndii was not at home. He dismounted, and went in to the princess; when they saw each other, their joy was so great that they fell to the ground. The princess said to him: 'O youth, why have you sought your doom? Against Kazha-Ndii you can do nothing.' But the young man would not hearken, and lifted her on to his horse.

As soon as they reached the gate, it creaked so loudly that a star fell from heaven. The door cried: 'Kazha-Ndii-Kerkun, where art thou? They have carried off your wife.' Kazha-Ndii heard this, and pursued them. When he was overtaking them, Kazha-Ndii's horse neighed so loudly that it stopped the princess's horse. The princess said to him: 'O youth, did I not tell you how it would be? Save yourself at least.' Then Kazha-Ndii rode up, cut the youth into pieces, and carried his wife back. The little dog came up, gathered the scattered fragments of the young man's body, put them in a bag, tied it to the saddle, mounted the horse, and took the body to the demis.

When the demis saw it they wept greatly, but their youngest brother blew the soul back into the pieces, and raised the youth to life. The prince arose, and again made ready to depart; the youngest demi said to him: 'Here is my three-legged

---

18 Kazha-Ndii-Kerkun means the swift demi.

horse, take him with you; if he do not help you there is no help to hope for.' The youth mounted the horse, came again to his princess, took her and put her on the horse. When he was riding out of the gate it creaked more loudly than before. Kazha-Ndii heard it and pursued them. As he was overtaking them, Kazha-Ndii's horse neighed, and the youth's horse slackened its speed. The young prince said to his horse: 'Why doe you this?' 'What can I do? If I had a fourth leg I might be victorious.' When Kazha-Ndii came near, the three-legged horse neighed so loudly that it stopped Kazha-Ndii's horse. Then the youth came up to him, brandished his sword, cut Kazha-Ndii into halves, put the princess on his horse, and they rode merrily away. They visited the demis and then went home.

THE STORY OF GERIA, THE POOR MAN'S SON

There was once a poor married man who had only one son; but this son was very handsome and strong, and his name was Geria[19]. Once the youth went out to hunt, and when he was coming home in the evening he met a woman with a jar going to the spring for water; he aimed an arrow at her, and broke the jar. The woman turned to him and said: 'If you are so warlike, instead of breaking my pot why do you not go and fetch the only sister of the twelve demis that dwell beyond the twelve mountains?' When he heard this, the youth's heart began to beat wildly for eagerness to see the maiden.

He went home and said to his parents: 'Get ready food to last me a year, and if I do not come back in that time set out to seek for me.' His parents would not consent, but said: 'We have no child but you, will you go away from us and perish?' They wept with one accord, but Geria heeded them not. So they got him provisions. They bade him farewell with sobs. Such wailing was there that the parting was known throughout the country side, yea, even to sun and moon, to heaven and earth, to the sea and the sands thereof. At last they blessed their son and let him go. He took with him a little dog, whose name was Mathicochi[20]. When they took leave one of another, they embraced, they kissed, and the youth sped on his way.

He went, he went, he went, he went as much as he could--week and week, week and fortnight, a year and three months—he went over six mountains. When he had crossed

19 This was originally footnoted as "Geria means little wolf".
20 Manticochi means "I also am a human being."

these six mountains everything round about him began to reel: trees and stones fell down and clattered into the valleys, but Geria was not hurt by them. Then, from beneath, there came to him a voice, saying: 'What kind of man art you to stand thus against me. Who can resist me but Geria, the poor man's son.' ''Tis I—Geria, the poor man's son.'

When she heard this, the Rokapi[21] went out to meet him, bowed herself, did great honor to him, and said: 'Where will you go?' The youth told her all. The Rokapi was moved with sorrow. Geria asked her: 'Why do you grieve?'--'For that I have seen many go there, but I have seen none come back.' But Geria heeded her not, and went on his way.

He went, he went, he went more than he could, and when he had crossed the other six mountains a still greater earthquake began. It turned out that this region belonged to the eldest sister of the Rokapis; but Geria showed no sign of fear. The Rokapi cried to him: 'What manner of man art you to resist my witchcraft? Are you Geria, the poor man's son?' He cried out to her: 'I am he.' The Rokapi at once went out to meet him, bowed, treated him with respect, and asked him: 'Where are you going?' Geria told her his plan, and this Rokapi too was distressed. Geria asked her why she grieved. She answered: 'Because I have seen many on their way there, but I have never seen one come back; albeit, I will do you one service, I give you my three-legged horse.' She called the horse, and said to him: 'As long as Geria lives serve him faithfully.' Geria bade her farewell, mounted the horse, and rode away

---

21 This was originally footnoted as "Rokapi in Georgian tales is an old woman of a demoniacal character, possessing enchanted castles and domains; sometimes the word simply means witch, and in ordinary conversation it is applied to an ugly, ill-natured, toothless old hag."

with his little dog Mathicochi.

He rode out into a great meadow, and came near the abode of the demis. When he looked upon the mead his heart was glad, and his eyes filled with tears, he bethought him of his home and its beautiful fields, he uttered a blessing to God the merciful. Then he urged his horse onward, at such speed that clouds of dust rose behind him. The youth said to himself: 'Lo, I am now in the unknown land!' Up he rode to the demis' gate, leaped from his horse, and tied it there.

He walked away a little, and then cried: 'Methinks I have not fastened my horse securely!' Back he went, tore up an oak by the roots, planted it with its branches downwards in the earth, and firmly tied his horse to it. Then the horse said: 'If you had not done this I should have fled home, but now do as I tell you, and all will be well. The demis are indoors; go to the meadow, there you will find a kettle, overturn it. Then betake yourself to the damsel, and get her to plight her troth to you.'

Geria went, kicked the kettle, turned it over three times, and left it upside down, then he went to the maiden, broke all the locks, and came to the room where she was. She was astonished, but the youth's bravery pleased her, and, to make a long story short, she promised to marry him. The youth went out merrily to the place where he had left his horse. There he quietly spent the night, and next morning the horse said: 'The demis have now gone out to the meadow; when they saw the kettle turned over they marvelled, for it usually takes all the twelve demis to turn over that kettle, and they said one to another: "Whatever we are commanded by him that turned over the kettle that must we do,"—now it is time for you to go there.' Geria went to the meadow.

As soon as the demis saw him, they all arose hastily, went

to meet him, bowed themselves, and said: 'What do you ask of us?' He answered: 'You must give me your sister to wife.' The demis said: 'We give her to you, but the Black King will not let you take her.' Geria answered: 'I fear no man,' so (not to lengthen unduly a long story) they made ready a banquet.

While the feast was still going on, in the morning, Geria looked out of the door, and saw a host of men in black apparel, who had been sent by the Black King. Geria mounted his horse, dashed into the midst and defeated them all; three only did he save alive, as messengers, and sent them to say to the Black King: ''Tis I that have done this, Geria, the poor man's son.'

The King was very wroth, and sent almost all his army against him. When Geria saw them, he bethought himself a little, but the horse said to him: 'Youth! This is nothing, look for still worse.' Geria struck the horse with his whip, attacked the host, and slew all but one; him he sent to bear the news. Upon this, the king went out of himself with rage: he summoned his devoted and loyal slave to whom he was wont to apply in all his difficulties, by name Qvamuritz Khami[22]; to him he committed all that was left of the army, and sent him out.

Geria arose and saw a sight, such a sight as I wish yours enemy may see. It pleased him not to see Qvamuritz Khami; but what could be done? The horse said to him: 'Youth! Yonder is he of whom I spake.' Geria crossed himself, gave thanks to God, bade his wife farewell, for he thought to die, and went out. First of all he slew the army, and then he began a single combat with Qvamuritz Khami.

Mounted they fought with maces, but the battle was not

22 Qyamuritz Khami translated to "he that has a star in his brow."

to the strong, for Qvamuritz Khami's soul was safe in other hands--how could he be killed? Qvamuritz Khami cried: 'O young man! Thus should you shoot!' and slayed him. When Geria was dead, the victor slaughtered all the demis, took Geria's wife, put her on her husband's horse, and carried her off to his master.

But she said to the king: 'I am the widow of such a man that I will not belong to a man like you; either do battle with me, and let the conqueror have his will, or give me leave to wear mourning for three months.' The king feared to fight with her, for she was of the demi race, so he gave her a respite of three months. When Geria was killed, his head rolled one way and his body another; his faithful dog Mathicochi went and put the two pieces together, and lay down to guard them.

While all these things had been happening, a year had passed, and when Geria's parents saw that he did not return, they set out to seek him. When they came to a narrow road, they saw that several snakes had met and were fighting, and all fell dead; then two great snakes crawled out, threw themselves into the river, swam out again and began to crawl over the dead snakes in various directions. They were all restored to life. Geria's parents wondered at the sight, and said one to the other: 'Let us take a little of this water.' They took a thimbleful of it.

When they approached, the little dog, Mathicochi, saw them, and ran to meet them; sadly he took them to the dead body. When the unhappy parents saw Geria dead, they both fell to the ground and sobbed bitterly; then they remembered that the mother of the unfortunate youth had the wonderful water with her. As soon as they sprinkled Geria with it he came to life, and said: 'Woe is me! What a long time I have slept!'

When he saw his parents, he was glad, but, remembering all that had befallen him, he again grew sad, and bade his parents farewell once more. They wept much, but, putting their trust in God, armed themselves with patience.

Geria set out for the land of the Black King, and when he came near, went into a great forest; as he entered, he heard a very great noise. He stopped, and there, on the road, he saw some one coming along, destroying all the forest as he went, tree fell on tree; he looked steadily, and saw a great boar rushing straight towards him; he threw himself on it, lifted it, and cast it three shoulders' lengths away from him; but they wrestled again, they wrestled, they wrestled, three whole days they wrestled. At last the youth was victorious, and tore the wild boar into halves. From the lacerated boar there leaped out a wild goat. When the youth killed the wild goat, there fell from it a little box; when he broke the box, three swallows flew from it—two of them he killed, the third he caught and kept.

At that time Qvamuritz Khami fell ill, the agony of death came upon him, for it turned out that this swallow was his soul. Geria killed the swallow, and Qvamuritz Khami died. After this, Geria went into the king's palace, and slew all therein excepting his wife. Her he took to his parents, whose patience and grief were exchanged for great joy. They all went home together.

THE PRINCE WHO
BEFRIENDED THE BEASTS

There was a king, and he had three sons. Once he fell ill, and became blind in both eyes. He sent his sons for a surgeon. All the surgeons agreed that there was a fish of a rare kind by the help of which the king might be cured. They made a sketch of the fish, and left it with the sick monarch.

The king commanded his eldest son to go and catch that fish in the sea. A hundred men with their nets were lost in the sea, but they could find nothing like the fish they sought. The eldest son came home to his father and said: 'I have found nothing.' This displeased the king, but what could he do? Then the second son set out, taking with him a hundred men also, but all his men were lost too, and he brought back nothing.

After this, the youngest brother went. He had recourse to cunning; he took with him a hundred kilas[23] of flour and one man. He came to the sea, and every day he scattered flour in the water, near the shore, until all the flour was used up; the fishes grew fat on the flour, and said: 'Let us do a service to this youth since he has enabled us to grow fat'; so, as soon as the youth threw a net into the sea, he at once drew out the rare fish he sought. He wrapped it up in the skirt of his robe, and went his way.

As he rode along, some distance from his companion, he heard a voice that said: 'O youth, I am dying!' But on looking round he saw no man, and continued his journey. After a short time, he again heard the same words. He looked round more carefully, but saw nothing. Then he glanced at the skirt of his robe, and saw that the fish had its mouth open, and was

---

23 A kila is a measure of flower, equivalent to about 40 pounds.

dying. The youth said to it: 'What do you want?' The fish answered: 'It will be better for you if you will let me go, some day I shall be of use to you.' The youth took it and threw it into the water, saying to his comrade: 'I hope you will not betray me.'

When he reached home, he told his father that he had been unsuccessful. Some time passed. Once the prince quarreled with his comrade, and the latter ran off and told the king how his son had deceived him. When the king heard this, he ordered his son to be taken away and killed. He was taken out, but when they were about to kill him, the youth entreated them, saying: 'What does it profit you if you slay me? If you let me go, 'twill be a good deed, and I shall flee to foreign lands.' The executioners took pity on him, and set him free; he thanked them, and departed.

He went, he went, he went, he went farther than anybody ever went--he came to a great forest. As he went through the forest, he saw a deer running, in a great state of alarm. The youth stopped, and fixed his gaze on it; then the deer came up and fell on its face before him. The youth asked: 'What ails you?' 'The prince pursues me, and on you depends my safety.' The youth took the deer with him and went on. A huntsman met him, and asked: 'Where are you leading the deer?' The youth replied: 'One king has sent it as a gift to another king, and, lo! I am taking it.' The youth thus saved the deer from death, and the deer said: 'A time will come when I shall save your life.'

The youth went on his way: he went, he went, he went, so far he went, good sir, that the 'three day colt' (of fable) could not go so far. He looked, and, lo! A frightened eagle perched on his shoulder, and said: 'Youth, on you depends my safety!' The youth protected it also from its pursuer. Then the eagle said to him: 'Some day I shall do you a service.'

The youth went on: he went through the forest, he went, he went, he went, he went farther than he could, he went a week, two weeks, a year and three months. Then he heard some fearful rumbling, roaring, thunder and lightning--something was coming through the forest, breaking down all the trees. A great jackal appeared, and ran up to the youth, saying: 'If you will you can protect me; the prince is pursuing me with all his army.' The youth saved the jackal, as he had saved the other animals. Then the jackal said: 'Some day I shall help you.'

The youth went on his way, and, when he was out of the wood, came to a town. In this town he found a castle of crystal, in the courtyard of which he saw a great number of young men, some dying and some dead. He asked the meaning of this, and was told: 'The king of this land has a daughter, a maiden queen; she has made a proclamation that she will wed him that can hide himself from her; but no man can hide himself from her, and all these men has she slain, for he that cannot hide himself from her is cast down from the top of the castle.'

When the youth heard this, he at once arose, and went to the maiden. They bowed themselves each to the other. The maiden asked him: 'Why have you come here?' The youth answered: 'I come for that which others have come for.' She immediately called her viziers together, and they wrote out the usual contract.

The youth went out from the castle, came to the seashore, sat down, and was soon buried in thought. Just then, something made a great splash in the sea, came and swallowed the youth, carried him into the Red Sea, there they were hidden in the depths of the sea, near the shore. The youth remained there all that night.

When the maiden arose next morning she brought her mirror and looked in it, but she found nothing in the sky, she looked on the dry land, and found nothing there, she looked at the sea--and then she saw the youth in the belly of the fish, which was hiding in the deep waters. After a short time, the fish threw up the youth on the place where it had found him. He went merrily to the maiden. She asked: 'Well, then, did you hide yourself?' 'Yes, I hid myself.' But the maiden told him where he had been, and how he got there, and added: 'This time I forgive you, for the cleverness you have shown.'

The youth set out again, and sat down in a field. Then something fell upon him, and took him up into the air, lifted him up into the sky, and covered him with its wing. When the maiden arose next morning, she looked in her mirror, she gazed at the mountain, she gazed at the earth, but she found nothing, she looked at the sky, and there she saw how the eagle was covering the youth. The eagle carried the youth down, and put him on the ground. He was joyful, thinking that the maiden could not have seen him; but when he came to her she told him all.

Then he fell into deep melancholy, but the maiden, being struck with wonder at his cunning in hiding himself, told him that she again forgave him. He went out again, and, as he was walking in the field, the deer came to him and said: 'Mount on my back.' He mounted, and the deer carried him away, away, away over all the mountains that were there, and put him in a lair. When the maiden arose next morning, she found him, and when he came back to her she said: 'Young man, it seems that you have many friends, but you can not hide yourself from me; yet this day also I forgive you.' The youth went sadly away; he had lost confidence.

When he sat down in the field, an earthquake began, the town shook, lightning flashed, thunder rolled, and when a thunderbolt had fallen, there leapt out from it his friend the gigantic jackal, and said to him: 'Fear not, O youth!' The jackal had recourse to its wonted cunning, it began to scrape at the earth: it dug, it dug, it dug, and burrowed right up to the place where the maiden dwelt, and then it said to the youth: 'Stay here, she will look at the sky, the mountain, the sea, and when she cannot find you she will break her mirror; when you hear this, then strike your head through the ground and come out.'

This advice, of course, pleased the youth. When the maiden arose in the morning, she looked at the sea, she found him not, she looked at the mountain, she looked at the sky, and still she could not see him, so she broke her mirror. Then the youth pushed his head through the floor, bowed, and said to the maiden: 'You are mine and I am yours!' They summoned the viziers, sent the news to the king, and a great feast began.

THE CUNNING OLD MAN
AND THE DEMI

There was once an old man. He might have worked but he was lazy. His children went out to the fields, but this old man sat by the fire, and if they did not show him great respect, he kept them out of the house. His daughters-in-law quarrelled with him, and ended by turning him out of the house. He begged of his eldest daughter-in-law, saying: 'Give me a jar of flour, an egg, and an awl, then I shall go away.' She gave him these things.

The old man went on day and night, and came to the bank of a stream; he looked over, and saw on the other side a demi, to whom he cried: 'Carry me across this river.' The demi answered: 'I shall not carry you, but you shall carry me across, or I shall turn you into dust.' The demi seized a stone, struck it on the rocky bank, and turned the great stone into powder. The old man also took his jar of flour, struck it on the rock, and dust arose. The demi was astonished, and said: 'How has he turned this stone into powder?' The demi took another stone, squeezed it in his hand, and said: 'I shall crush you like this stone.' Then the old man took out the egg, squeezed it, and when the moisture began to ooze out, the demi was alarmed: he came over the stream, took the old man on his shoulder, and carried him across.

In the middle of the stream, the demi said to the old man: 'How light you art!' The old man answered: 'I am holding on to the sky with one hand, if I let go, you wouldst fall under my weight.' The demi said: 'Just leave go for a moment.' The old man took out the awl, and stuck it in the demi's neck. The demi cried: 'Lay hold of the sky again!' The old man put the awl in his pocket.

When they had reached the other side, the demi said to the old man: 'I shall drive in game, and you can meet it here.' So the demi went and drove in the game. The old man was afraid of wild beasts, and hid himself in the forest, where he found a dead redbreast[24]. When the demi returned, he asked: 'What have you done with the game?' The old man replied: 'You did not drive the game properly, or how could any beast that walks on earth escape from me, that could catch this bird on the wing?'

The demi went and killed two deer, two wild goats, two boars, two hares; some he boiled, some he roasted, he made ready two kilas of millet, two cocas of wine, and said: 'Let us sit down and eat.' The old man said: 'Make me a bridge over this river, there will I drink.' The demi built him a little bridge, on which he seated himself. The demi gave him one deer, one wild goat, one boar, one hare, one kila of millet, one coca of wine, and then sat down near him in the field. The demi ate, but the old man threw the food into the river. The demi thought the old man was eating everything, and was afraid, thinking: 'It would seem that he can eat more than I can.' Lower down the stream, wolves caught and ate the meat the old man threw away. The old man asked for another deer. The demi brought it, and the old man threw it in the water. The demi did not know this. The old man said: 'I have had a snack this evening.'

Next day, the demi invited the old man to his house. They went there. The demi went out alone to hunt. He met a wolf and a jackal, and said to them: 'Come and hunt with me. To my house there has come a guest who can eat ten deer and

---

24 A redbreast probably refers to a red-breasted finch.

wild goats; yesterday evening we had two deer, but they were a mere snack to him.' The wolf and the jackal said to the demi: 'You guest did not eat one of them, he threw everything into the river, we caught it and ate it, the old man ate nothing.' The demi said to the wolf and the jackal: 'Then let us go and expose this old man's fraud.'

There went with the demi nine wolves and jackals, to give evidence against the old man. The old man looked out, and saw the demi coming along in front, with the wolves and jackals behind him. The old man cried to the demi: 'Do you not owe me more than ten wolves and jackals?' The wolves and jackals exchanged glances, and said: 'It would seem that this demi has betrayed us.' They threw themselves on the demi and turned him into dust.

SANARTIA

There was once a king who reached old age without having a son. When he was very old, his wife at last bore him a son. The child was called Sanartia[25]; he grew up, and became very good and very clever, so that he understood everything that took place among earthly beings, wherever they were; but he did not obey his mother. She therefore hated him, and said to the king, her husband: 'Since this boy will not obey his mother in anything, take him and throw him into the great deep sea.'

The king was much distressed, but he did as his wife asked. The youth guessed what his parents were talking about, but he showed no resistance. After this, his father said: 'Let us go and look at the town.' Then the youth said: 'Papa, give me a little money.' His father gave him money, and they went to see the town. When they arrived, the boy bought a little axe, knives, needle, thread, flint and tinder.

When they were on their way home, they came near the sea; the boy pulled up an oak tree, and carried it on his shoulder. The father was the first to see the sea, and when they were on the shore he said to his son: 'Come here, and see what a big fish I shall show you.' When the son came up to look, his father cast him into the great sea, together with the tree he carried. A fish swallowed the youth; his father turned and went home.

In the sea, the youth kindled a fire in the fish's belly, cut caviar out of it, roasted and ate it. On the caviar from this fish the youth lived thirty years, in the belly of that fish. Then, his firewood, flint and tinder being well-nigh exhausted, he made a very big fire. When the fish felt the heat, it leaped up and fell on the dry land. The youth said: 'I will cut open the fish's

25 Sanartia means "desired," or "longed for".

belly, and see—if it is in the water, I shall sew it up again, if it is ashore, I shall make a hole and get out.' He cut a little, and saw that it was on land. Then he cut a large opening, came out of the fish, made a fire, cut flesh from the fish, roasted it, and ate it.

Just then, there passed a prince, on his way to marry a maiden, and he saw the other prince coming out of the fish. The prince who was going to seek his bride, sent a man to the youth to ask him to make way, for he was sitting in the road, and there was no other road for horsemen. But Sanartia would not move. Then the prince himself rode up, and asked: 'Who are you?' Sanartia told him the name of the king, his father. Then the prince invited him, saying: 'I go to marry a wife; ride with me.' Sanartia agreed, and they went together to the appointed place.

When they came near, they sent on a man to the king, who was master of the country, asking him to give his daughter in marriage to the prince. The king agreed, and sent to say: 'If the prince succeeds in performing two exploits, I shall fulfill his wish; but to do these deeds is both hard and perilous: the princess throws a great lump of lead as far as a gun will carry a bullet, the suitor must throw it back again to the place where the princess is standing.' The suitor for the maiden's hand sent and said: 'I will do this.'

He went and stood in the place the maiden pointed out to him. She threw a piece of lead which fell at the place where the prince stood; he was not only unable to throw the lead, but could not even lift it from the ground; then his comrade, the other prince, Sanartia, took up the lead and threw it for him. The piece of lead went much farther than the maiden had thrown it.

This exploit having been performed, the prince had another to do: mistaking Sanartia for the suitor, they took him to a wilderness where there was a castle, and in it dwelt Ocho-Kochi[26]. They opened the door of the castle, and let in the prince, saying: 'This Ocho-Kochi will kill the young man.' He spent that night in the castle.

When he was preparing to sleep, Ocho-Kochi came to him and wished to kill him, but Sanartia was very strong, he seized Ocho-Kochi, threw him on the ground, and beat him with all his might. When he had beat him soundly, he said to him: 'Go and stand at the gate as watchman.' So he went and watched till dawn.

In the morning, the king, the maiden's father, sent his vizier, saying: 'Find out what the prince and Ocho-Kochi are doing.' When the vizier came to the door, Ocho-Kochi called out from the inside: 'Master sleeps, wake him not, or he will beat me.' The vizier made no reply to Ocho-Kochi, but went back and told the king what he had heard.

The king was amazed, he set out for the castle, and said to Ocho-Kochi: 'Open the door to me.' But Ocho-Kochi replied: 'Master will kill me.' Just then, Sanartia awoke, and said to Ocho-Kochi: 'Open the door for him.' He immediately opened the door, and let in the king. Then the king and Sanartia went away together. The king wished to marry him to his daughter, but Sanartia went away secretly; he dressed the prince, his companion, in his clothes, and sent him in his place to the king; as soon as he arrived he was wedded to the princess. Afterwards Sanartia visited him as a friend.

---

26 Ocho-Kochi, literally, 'the goat-man,' occupies an important place in Mingrelian mythology. He is a satyr, a wild man of the woods, represented as an old man with a long beard, his body covered with hair.

If they had known that Sanartia had performed these exploits they would not have given the princess to the other prince. But a handmaiden at the court found out the secret somehow, that Sanartia had done the deeds, and the princess's husband had done nothing. One evening the handmaiden told the princess how Sanartia had cheated her and married her to another man; she was angry, and that same night, after Sanartia had lain down to sleep, she went and cut off his leg at the knee.

Sanartia did not die of the wound, but went away to another land, and became friendly with a one-handed man, and they lived together in the house of the latter. Afterwards they built a house in common, and moved into it. Sanartia took a maiden, and kept her with him as nurse[27]. The two friends went out to hunt, and stayed in the forest all night. At home there was nobody but the maiden.

Meantime there came a demi, who sucked the maiden's breast and then went away. When Sanartia and his friend came home, the girl told them what had happened. Sanartia left his friend and the girl at home, and said to them: 'If the demi comes, take him and keep him till I come back.' The demi came, but the man was afraid to lay hold of him; and the demi went away again. As soon as Sanartia came in, he asked his friend and his nurse: 'What did you do?' They answered: 'The demi came, but we could not take him, and he went away again.'

---

27 The word translated 'nurse' is dzidze, which means not only a nurse but any woman, married or single, who has been adopted into relationship by the ceremony of a man taking her breast between his teeth. This creates a degree of kinship inferior only to that between mother and son. The custom still exists in Mingrelia.

Next day Sanartia stayed at home, and sent his friend to hunt. The demi came that night also, but as soon as Sanartia saw him he met him at the door, and when the demi came in, Sanartia seized him and threw him to the ground, then he told the nurse to bring a rope, with which he bound him tightly. He took out his dagger, and was about to cut him in pieces, but the demi entreated him, saying: 'Slay me not, and I will heal you of all infirmities.' Sanartia hearkened to the demi's prayers, and said: 'If you wilt restore my leg which was cut off I will let you go, otherwise I slay you.'

The demi pledged his word to heal him, and led him to a great river, saying: 'Put you leg therein and it will be sound.' But Sanartia did not yet believe the demi, so he ordered him to bring a dry stick, and said: 'Put this stick in the water, and if it becomes green and bears leaves then will I put in my leg, otherwise I will not.' The stick was put in the water, but it came out as dry as before.

Then Sanartia was angry, and wished to kill the demi, but again he entreated, saying: 'There is still another healing stream.' So he took him to the other stream, and as soon as Sanartia put in his leg it was made whole and sound like the other leg. After this, he did not kill the demi, but let him go free; he made the demi heal his one-handed friend, whom he wedded to his nurse. He left them there, and set out for his father's house.

But when he reached it, nobody knew him. Next day he secretly mounted his father's horse, and went to the place where he had married the prince to the princess. On the road he saw a swineherd; when he approached, he recognised in him his old friend the prince. When he questioned him, the swineherd replied: 'As soon as you hadst gone hence they made me a swineherd.' Sanartia drew out his sword, gave it to him, and said: 'Kill all the swine but three, and wound those three; then drive the three home, I shall be there, ready to punish anybody who is angry with you.' The swineherd did as Sanartia told him, and in the evening drove the three swine into the king's courtyard.

Sanartia came to the palace earlier, but they did not recognise him. When the swineherd drove in his swine, his wife was about to beat him, saying: 'Why hast you lost the swine.' But at that moment Sanartia appeared before the princess, was angry with her, and said: 'If you wert a good woman you wouldst not make you husband feed swine.'... They knew at once that it was Sanartia, and were much amazed, saying: 'His leg was cut off at the knee, how has he replaced his leg?' Sanartia ordered them to bring the princess's husband: he made her wash him well with her own hands, bring clothes, and dress him in noble apparel. When Sanartia was leaving for home, he called the princess and her parents, and said to them: 'If you do not treat the prince as becomes his rank, I shall come at once, and it will fare ill with you.' He took leave of them all and went home.

THE SHEPHERD JUDGE

In a certain land, there was once a king who had four viziers to judge the people. Once these judges uttered a remarkable sentence. At that time there came to the king a certain shepherd, who spoke in a manner that pleased the king, so he commanded the viziers: 'Show this shepherd the sentence you pronounced.' When the shepherd had examined the decree of the viziers, it did not please him; he took it and altered it from beginning to end.

When the king saw this, he said to the shepherd: 'Since you are so skilled in judging, you should be a judge.' The shepherd refused, and said: 'As long as I have eyes I cannot judge, if you put out both my eyes then I will be a judge.' Finally he persuaded them to put out his eyes. They built him a great, fine house, they gave him scribes, furnished him with everything befitting his office, and made the shepherd supreme judge.

He began to do justice in such an upright manner that people flocked to him from every side. Everybody went to him for justice: great and small, master and servant, old and young, clergy and laity, friend and enemy—in a word, all who had suits with anybody came to him, every one praised and blessed his decisions.

Once there came to him a man and a woman. The man said to the judge: 'I came to this woman's house on a mule; a calf accompanied my mule. When I tied up the mule, the calf began to suck its breast. The woman, seeing this, ran out, seized the calf, and began to grumble at me, saying it was her calf, and asking how it came to be with my mule. I withstood her with all my might, but it was of no avail. She wished to drag away the calf, but I would not allow it, I would not give up my property to her; we quarreled, and now we have come before you—in God's name judge between us!' Thus he spoke in person to the judge, but secretly he sent him a large bribe and a message, saying: 'Take this money, and put me not to shame before this woman.'

But the judge would not tamper with the scales of justice, and sent to tell the man: 'How can I take the calf from the woman by force, if justice do not demand it?' The judge asked the woman: 'What do you say?' The woman replied: 'My lord, this man rode up to my house on a mule; I had nothing in the world but one calf and its mother, which I loved; my calf went up to this man's mule, caressed it, and took hold of it with its snout, as if it were going to suck its breast. The man, seeing this, thought: 'I shall certainly take away this calf with me.' He dragged it home, but, of course, I could not allow this—everyone extols your equity, I too am come to your door, and trust you will not suffer me to be trampled down by injustice.'

When the judge had heard both sides, he pronounced the following decision: 'Since a mule never bore offspring and never will, it is still less possible that a mule should bring forth a calf. Let the calf therefore be taken from the man, and given to the woman who owns the cow, the mother of the calf.' This judgment pleased everybody in the highest degree. And God was merciful to this good judge: by means of the kerchief of that woman his eyes were made whole, and he saw. After this he saw with both eyes, but till the day of his death he judged uprightly; when he died he went to heaven.

THE PRIEST'S
YOUNGEST SON

There was once a priest who had three sons. On the day of his death, the priest said to his sons: 'When I die, let each of you read the Book of Psalms over me for one night.' But the elder sons did not do as their father had requested, only the youngest read the Book of Psalms over him. That night his father appeared, and gave him a horse. Next night he again read the Book of Psalms over his father in his brothers' place. His father again appeared, and gave him another horse, which he resolved to give to his younger brother. On the third night he again read the Book of Psalms. His father brought him a third horse, gave the young man his blessing, and departed.

At that time, a princess was to be married to any man whose horse could jump up to the castle, so that its rider could kiss that maiden-queen. Many princes came to woo her, but none of their horses could leap up to the castle. Then the priest's youngest son mounted the horse his father had given him, and rode up to the royal palace; he struck the horse with his switch, and made it jump, but it could only go one third of the way up to the castle. Next day he mounted another horse, and made it jump, it went two thirds of the height of the castle. The third day he came on the third horse, and made it jump; it jumped right up to the top of the castle; the youth kissed the princess, and they married him to her. After this the priest's son went home.

At this time the queen, his mother-in-law, fell ill; she sent for her son-in-law, and said to him: 'Between the white sea and the black sea there feeds a doe, they tell me that its milk will do me good; if you can get it for me I shall recover, if not, I must die.' Then the youth mounted his horse and went forth. He rode between the seas, milked the doe, brought its milk to his mother-in-law, gave it to her to drink, and healed her.

MINGRELIAN PROVERBS

1. *Turn to the right, or turn to the left, it will all be one in the end.*

2. *The rat that came from outside, drove out the house-born rat.*

3. *Fight for the outlying village, if you want the one nearer home.*

4. *Wish your neighbor to have an ox, and God will send it to you.*

5. *The wolf was abused as wolfish, while the jackal ate up the flock.*

6. *The hen scratched and scratched till she dug up a knife, with which her own throat was afterwards cut.*

7. *The road runs where an old road ran, the river flows in the bed of a former river.*

8. *'Give me room to stand,' said the bull, 'and I Shall make myself enough room to lie.'*

9. *If the bear conquers you—then call him Papa.*[28]

10. *The dog took fright at a wolf, and barked all year round at a stump.*

11. *Who ever heard of a fish being prized, as long as it stayed in the stream?*

12. *They shot at the ripe fruit, but the green one fell.*

13. *Leave a good deed on a stone by the way, and you will find it again after many a day.*[29]

14. *I say it—but whether it happens or not has noth-*

---

28 Compare to the Talmud: 'If the fox is king bow before him'
29 i.e., "Cast you bread on the waters."

ing to do with me.

15. *Eat and drink up whatever is yours, but cross yourself over all that's mine.*

16. *Who killed me?—My brother. Who brought me back to life?—My brother.*

17. *The well-doer receives not good in return.*

18. *The truthful man is always duped.*

19. *My father I love, my mother I love—But myself I prefer before all.*

20. *A heart-kiss is better than a lip-kiss.*

21. *If you hast not eaten pepper, why does you mouth burn?*

22. *A disease that one sees, will not kill; It is hidden sores do the most ill.*

23. *Our granny has no teeth, so she likes not others' teeth to see.*

24. *He has forgotten the soul of his father, so he swears by the soul of his grandfather.*

25. *Gold is good, but if you have it not, of what use is it to you?*

26. *Better is copper of yours own than gold that is another's.*

27. *Of what use is light to him that is blind?*

28. *If you are brave, do not lament the bluntness of your sword.*

THE STRONG MAN AND
THE DWARF

There came from far-off lands a strong man who had nowhere met his match, and challenged any one in the whole kingdom to wrestle with him. The king gathered his folk together, but, to his wonder, could not for a long time find anybody ready to face the strong man, till, at last, there stood forth a weak insignificant-looking dwarf, who offered to wrestle with the giant.

Haughtily looking down on his adversary, the giant carelessly turned away, thinking that he was befooled. But the dwarf asked that his strength should be put to the proof before the struggle began.

The giant angrily seized a stone, and, clasping it in his fingers, squeezed moisture out of it.

The dwarf cunningly replaced the stone by a sponge of the same appearance, and squeezed still more moisture out of it.

The giant then took another stone, and threw it so violently on the ground that it became dust.

The dwarf took a stone, hid it under the ground, and threw on the ground a handful of flour, to the great astonishment of the giant.

Stretching forth his hand to the dwarf, the giant said: 'I never expected to find so much strength in such a small man, I will not wrestle with you; but give me your hand in token of friendship and brotherhood.'

After this, the giant asked the dwarf to go home with him. But first he asked the dwarf why he had not pressed his hand in a brotherly manner. The dwarf replied that he was unable to moderate the force of his pressure, and that more than one man had already died from the fearful force of his hand. The new brothers then set out together. On their way to the giant's house, they came to a stream that had to be cross.

The dwarf, fearing to be carried away by the current, told the strong man that he was suffering from belly-ache, and did not therefore wish to go into the cold water, so he asked to be carried over.

In the midst of the stream, the strong man, with the dwarf on his shoulders, suddenly stopped and said: 'I have heard that strong people are heavy, but I do not feel you on my shoulders. Tell me how this is, for God's sake.'

'Since we have become brothers,' replied the dwarf, 'I have no right to press with all my weight upon you, and did I not support myself by holding on to the sky with one hand, you could never carry me.'

But the strong man, wishing to test his strength, asked the dwarf to drop his hand for a moment, whereupon the dwarf took from his pocket two nails, and stuck the sharp points of them in the shoulders of the strong man.

The giant could not endure the pain, and begged the dwarf to lighten his burden at once, i.e. to lay hold of heaven with one hand again.

When they had reached the other side, the two new friends soon came to the strong man's house. The giant, wishing to give a dinner to the dwarf, proposed that they should share the work of getting it ready, that one of them should take the bread out of the oven, while the other went to the cellar for wine.

The dwarf saw in the oven an immense loaf that he could never have lifted, so he chose to go to the cellar for wine. But when he had descended, he was unable even to lift the weights on the top of the jars, so, thinking that by this time the giant would have taken the loaf out of the oven, he cried: 'Shall I bring up all the jars?'

The giant, alarmed lest the dwarf should spoil his whole year's stock of wine, by digging the jars out of the ground, where they were buried, rushed down into the cellar, and the dwarf went upstairs.

But great was the astonishment of the dwarf when he found that the bread was still in the oven, and that he must take it out, willy-nilly. He succeeded with difficulty in dragging a loaf to the edge of the oven, but then he fell with the hot bread on top of him, and, being unable to free himself, was almost smothered.

Just then the giant came in, and asked what had happened. The dwarf replied: 'As I told you this morning, I am suffering from a stomach-ache, and, in order to soothe the pain, I applied the hot loaf as a plaster.' Then the giant came up, and said: 'Poor fellow! How do you feel now, after your plaster?' 'Better, thank God,' replied the dwarf, 'I feel so much better that you can take off the loaf.' The giant lifted the loaf, and the two then sat down to dinner. Suddenly the giant sneezed so hard that the dwarf was blown up to the roof, and seized a beam, so that he should not fall down again. The giant looked up with astonishment, and asked: 'What does this mean?' The dwarf angrily replied: 'If you do such a vulgar thing again I shall pull this beam out and break it over your stupid head.' The giant made humble excuses, and promised that he would never sneeze again during dinnertime; he then brought a ladder by which the dwarf came down...

THE GRASSHOPPER
AND THE ANT

The grasshopper and the ant became friends, and entered into a compact of brotherhood, promising never to separate. They then set out on a journey, forgetful of the proverb that 'footman and horseman can never be comrades.' Of the truth of this they had a proof on the very first day of their travels, for, chancing to come to a stream that they had to cross, the grasshopper jumped over, while the poor ant was carried away by the stream.

The grasshopper thought, for a moment, how he could save his drowning companion, and then cried: 'Catch hold of something, and I shall run and get help.'

The bright idea struck him of applying to the sow for one of her bristles, to which the ant could attach herself while he pulled her out of the water.

The sow answered: 'Brother grasshopper, you know the proverb, "hand washes hand"; for three days I have eaten nothing, and am I to let people pull bristles out of me for nothing? Feed me with acorns, and then you can have as many bristles as you like.'

The grasshopper hurried off to the oak and said: 'Oak, oak, give me acorns, I give the acorns to the sow, the sow gives me a bristle, and with the bristle I save my drowning comrade.'

The oak answered:

'Those thievish jays give me no rest, they pull off my acorns; keep them off.'

The grasshopper ran to the jays, and said:

'Jays! leave the oak, and the oak will give me acorns, the

acorns I give to the sow, the sow gives me a bristle, and with the bristle I save my drowning comrade.'

The jays answered:

'The kites pursue us; go and drive them off.'

The grasshopper ran to the kites, and said:

'Kites! leave the jays, and the jays will leave the oak, the oak will give me acorns, the acorns I give to the sow, the sow gives me a bristle, and with the bristle I save my drowning comrade.'

The kites answered:

'We are hungry; bring us chickens.'

The grasshopper ran to the hen, and said:

'Hen, give me chickens. The chickens I shall give to the kites, the kites leave the jays, the jays leave the oak, the oak gives acorns, the acorns I give to the sow, the sow gives me a bristle, with the bristle I save my drowning comrade.'

The hen replied:

'Feed me with millet.'

The grasshopper hastened to the barn:

'Barn, give me millet, the millet I give to the hen, the hen gives me chickens, the chickens I give to the kites, the kites leave the jays, the jays leave the oak, the oak gives acorns, the acorns I give to the sow, the sow gives me a bristle, and with the bristle I save my drowning comrade.'

The barn replied:

'The rats have the mastery over me, they gnaw me on every side; send them away.' The grasshopper ran to the rats:

'Rats! go away from the barn, and the barn will give me millet, the millet I give to the hen, the hen gives me chickens, the chickens I give to the kites, the kites leave the jays, the jays leave the oak, the oak gives acorns, the acorns I give to the sow, the sow gives me a bristle, and with the bristle I save my drowning friend.'

The rats replied:

'The cats give us no peace; send them away.'

The grasshopper went to the cats:

'Cats! go away from the rats, and the rats will leave the barn, the barn will give millet, the millet I give to the hen, the hen gives me chickens, the chickens I give to the kites, the kites leave the jays, the jays leave the oak, the oak gives acorns, the acorns I give to the sow, the sow gives me a bristle, and with this bristle I shall save my drowning comrade.'

The cats replied:

'Feed us with milk.'

The grasshopper ran to the cow:

'Cow! give me milk, the milk I shall give to the cats, the cats will leave the rats alone, the rats will leave the barn,' etc., etc.

The cow replied:

'Feed me with grass.'

The grasshopper applied to the earth, and said:

'O earth! give me grass, the grass I shall give to the cow, the cow will give me milk, the milk I shall give to the cats, then the cats will leave the rats alone, and the rats will leave the barn, the barn will give me millet, the millet I shall give to the hen, the hen will give me chickens, the chickens I shall give to the kites, then the kites will leave the jays, and the jays will leave the oak, the oak will give me acorns, the acorns I shall give to the sow, the sow will give me a bristle, and with this bristle I shall save my drowning friend.'

The earth gave the grass... and finally the grasshopper obtained the bristle, and hastened with it to his drowning friend, but, to his astonishment, the ant was quite dead when he pulled him out. This story teaches that help is only valuable when it is given in time, that the earth alone refuses not to yield her gifts to him that asks, and that all other things exist only by reciprocal services.

THE COUNTRYMAN
AND THE MERCHANT

A countryman caught a pheasant, and was carrying it home to cook it for himself and his wife.

Suddenly the pheasant spoke like a man, and said: 'Let me go, goodman, and I shall repay you.'

The countryman was astonished, and asked:

'What could you do for me?'

The pheasant replied: 'You are an old man, and must soon die; when you are dead, I shall gather together all the birds of the air, and follow you to the grave. Since the world began, no king ever had such an honor paid to him at his funeral.'

The countryman was pleased at the offer, and set the pheasant free. When he reached home, he told his wife what had happened, and, although she scolded him at first for letting the bird go, yet she was pleased when the pheasant sent, every morning, birds to ask after the old man's health.

A happy thought soon occurred to the wife, and she said to her husband: 'Listen to me, we are almost dying of hunger, and we have a good chance of getting plenty of food. Pretend that you are dead; I shall begin to cry, and all the birds will come to your funeral, I shall entice them into our cottage, shut the doors and windows; we can knock them down with sticks, and thus lay in a store of food to last us for a long time.'

So the countryman covered himself with a sheet, and lay down, while his wife went outside and wept loudly.

A hoopoe flew down, and asked after her husband's health; when the wife announced his death, the hoopoe at once flew away, and, within an hour, there flew into the yard, in long lines, some thousands of pheasants, the same number of doves, snipe, quails, woodcock, etc., and even eagles, kites, hawks, etc.

Some of the birds settled in the cottage, some in the barn, some in the stable, some in the yard, and the rest, for which there was no room, remained in serried ranks in the air.

Then the wife shut the doors, and, with her husband, set about killing the birds; only those that were outside escaped.

In the evening, there came a merchant, and asked to be allowed to spend the night in the cottage. At supper, the merchant saw a great abundance of game of all kinds, and asked the countryman how such luxury was within the reach of a poor man. The countryman replied: 'I have a cat of a famous breed, which has never yet failed me. When I want game for my table, I tell her what kind of birds I should like, and how many, and she goes into the forest and gets them. I do not know what was the matter with her last night, but see! She went into the wood of her own will, and killed all the birds in the neighborhood, and brought them to us.' The countryman then showed a whole heap of dead game.

The merchant at once began to bargain with the countryman for the cat, and finally purchased it for a large sum.

When the merchant reached home, he went about his business, and told his wife that he would not leave her any money for housekeeping, for she had only to give her orders, and the cat would bring all sorts of game for food. But when he came in, he was astonished to find that his wife had eaten nothing, the cat had brought no birds, but had even stolen what was in the house already. So he went back to ask the countryman about it.

The countryman saw him coming, filled a pot with millet and hung it over the fire. He then sat down near it, put a grain of millet in the palm of his hand, and began to wash it. The merchant came in and stood by him; the countryman pretended not to see the merchant, muttered an incantation, and dropped the grain into the pot. Then he stirred it with a spoon, and behold the pot was full. The merchant did not know whether to quarrel with the countryman or to get this magic pot from him.

'What is this you have done to me?' said he. 'Your cat is useless, it brings nothing, and steals what we have.'

'Have you been feeding it with roast meat? I forgot to warn you that you must not do this.'

'Well, it is my fault then,' said the merchant. 'But will you sell me that pot?'

'I have already lost my famous cat. It is not likely that I shall now let you have this pot, in which I can make a dish of porridge with only one grain.'

However, they began bargaining, and at last the countryman sold his pot for a large sum. When the merchant reached home, he consoled his wife by telling her that from one barleycorn she could now make as much porridge as she wanted; he then set out again. When he returned, his wife complained that the pot was of no use. So he called again on the countryman, to ask for an explanation.

The countryman, foreseeing that the merchant would come, got two hares exactly alike, and tied ribbons of the same color round their necks. He left one hare at home, and took the other out into the fields with him. He told his wife that if the merchant came, she was to send him out to the field, and in an hour bring him a dinner consisting of two boiled fowls, a roast turkey, ten eggs, wine, and bread.

The merchant came, and the woman sent him to the field where her husband was working. In reply to the reproaches of the merchant, the countryman said: 'You have probably made some stupid mistake with the pot as you did with the cat. But let us sit down and dine while we talk it over, for I cannot suffer you to come to me without feeding you.' The merchant looked round and said: 'How can we get anything to eat out here in the fields?'

The peasant went to a bush, untied the hare, and said to it: 'Run at once, little hare, to my wife, and tell her to come with you and bring us a pair of fowls, a roast turkey, ten eggs, wine, and bread.'

The hare ran off as fast as it could. It is easy to understand the astonishment of the merchant when the woman came with the hare, bringing all that the man had ordered. When they had eaten, the merchant said: 'You have cheated me about the cat and the pot, but I forgive you if you let me have the hare.' The countryman refused at first, but finally agreed to sell the hare for a large sum.

On his way home with the hare, the merchant met some friends whom he asked to sup with him, but seeing that he would not arrive until it was late, he ordered the hare to run and tell his wife that he was coming with some guests, and that she was to prepare supper. When he and his friends reached home, they found the house quite dark, and had difficulty in rousing the wife from her sleep. She told him that no hare had been there, and that she did not know what he was talking about.

The merchant was now furious, and determined to punish the countryman severely. But the countryman guessed what would happen, and arranged with his wife what should be done. He took the intestine of a small calf, filled it with blood, and tied it round his wife's neck, telling her to cover it up with a kerchief. The merchant came in, and without saying a word rushed at the countryman, who, in his turn, attacked his wife, accusing her of being the guilty party, and with a knife pierced the intestine under her throat. She fell on the ground, and pretended that she was dying. The merchant was alarmed, and cried: 'What have you done, you wretched man? I would willingly have lost the money rather than have this innocent blood shed.' The countryman answered: 'That is my affair. Though I have killed my wife I can raise her to life again.' 'I believe you no longer,' said the merchant, 'but if you perform this miracle I shall forgive you all.' The countryman approached his wife with the knife in his hand, muttered something, and his wife opened her eyes, and, to the surprise of the merchant, rose up.

The merchant bought the wonderful knife, saying that his wife, too, needed a lesson sometimes. When the merchant reached home, his wife asked where he had been. He told her to be silent and mind her own business. 'If you are not quiet I will cut your throat.' The woman looked at him with astonishment, and wondered whether he had gone out of his mind. The merchant threw down his wife, and cut her throat. All the neighbors flocked in, and raised a great cry. The merchant said: 'What if I have killed my wife? I can bring her to life again.' The neighbors stood by while he muttered the invocations he had learnt, but he could not raise her. Then he flew to the countryman, tied his hands, and dragged him into the forest, saying: 'I wish to prolong your sufferings, and will not kill you at once. I shall starve you, drag you about in the woods, and, when I have worn you out with tortures, I shall throw you into the sea.' On the road there was a town, in which a king had just died, and his funeral was then taking place. Having bound the countryman to a tree in the depths of the forest, the merchant returned to the town to see the royal funeral. Just then, a shepherd happened to drive his flock near the tree to which the countryman was tied. Seeing the shepherd a little way off, the countryman began to shout: 'I will not be king! I will not be king! No! No! No!' The shepherd came up and asked what was wrong. The countryman replied: 'You know, brother, that the king is dead in the town: they want me to take his place, but I will not, for I have been king twice, and know what it is. Ah, brother! one has so many cares, so much work, that one's head swims. I had rather be tied to this tree than consent to be king.' The shepherd thought for a moment, and replied: 'I, brother, would give anything in the world to have a trial of the life of a king.' 'I gladly give you my place, but, so that people may not know, put on my clothes, and I shall bind you to the tree, and by to-morrow you shall be king.' The shepherd gladly gave him his flock, and took his place at the tree.

As soon as the countryman was free, he drove away the flock.

When it was quite dark, the merchant appeared, loosed his victim, and drove him on. When they came to the steep seashore, the shepherd saw that the merchant wished to drown him, and cried: 'Do not drown me! I had rather consent to be king.' The merchant thought his prisoner had lost his wits through fatigue and ill-treatment; without more ado he threw him into the sea.

A fortnight later, the merchant was travelling on business, when he met on the road the same countryman whom he, as he thought, had drowned, and who was now driving a flock. 'What do I see!' cried the merchant. 'Are you there? Did I not drown you in the sea?'

'My benefactor!' replied the countryman. 'I wish you would drown me again. You cannot imagine what a quantity of cattle there is down there at the bottom of the sea. It is a pity I had no stick with me, for I could not drive out more than these with my hands.'

The merchant besought the countryman, saying: 'You have ruined me. The cat, the pot, the hare, the knife, have all cost money; thanks to you, I am a beggar and a widower. If you remember the place where I threw you into the sea, drown me there, but let me have a stick, so that I may repair my fortune.' To get rid of the troublesome merchant, the countryman agreed to fulfill his request, and so drowned him with a very long switch in his hand.

THE KING AND THE SAGE

Once upon a time, there reigned in one of the realms of the East a shah named Ali, a man of amiable and merry character. Ali was much beloved by his subjects, and he too loved them with all his heart. The shah played with them as if they had been his children; he gave them festivals, arranged competitions, and gave prizes for the best poetical productions, etc. The shah was skilled in the famous literature of Arabia, and was thought to be a learned man; besides this, he was a wit and a joker, and loved to set his folk merry riddles to guess: prizes were given to the successful. Once the servants of the shah made known to the people, that Ali had promised three hundred pieces of gold to him who should ask his majesty such a question that the answer must inevitably be: That is Impossible.

This announcement created great excitement, and men, women, and children all alike set themselves to think out such a question. The day of the competition dawned at last, and the vast square before the palace was crowded with a curious throng. At the appointed hour, Shah Ali appeared, surrounded by a brilliant guard, and music filled the air. After greeting his folk, the shah sat down on a throne, opposite the platform on which the candidates were to stand while they asked the shah their questions. Heralds gave out the challenge, and a wit of the town mounted the rostrum and loudly said: 'Shah! A courier has just galloped into the town and told me a most astonishing piece of news, to wit, that at dawn this morning, twenty versts[30] from your capital, the moon fell from the sky to the ground, and burned two and twenty villages to ashes.'

30 A verst is a Russian measure of length, equivalent to about 1km.

The shah meditated a moment, and then replied: 'That is possible.' The town wit got down, amid the laughter of the people.

His place was taken by a courtier, the shah's body-surgeon, who shouted: 'Most illustrious Shah! In your harem a most astounding event has just happened--your first wife, your beloved Zuleika, has just given birth to a sucking-pig covered with bristles.' The shah considered, and then replied: 'That is possible.' The doctor fled in shame, and the people laughed more loudly than before.

After the doctor came an astrologer, who said: 'Most noble Shah! In observing the courses of the stars I have discovered a woeful piece of news; an awful fate awaits you. O King, you will soon have horns like a goat, and claws like a panther, you will lose the power of speech, and flee from us into the woods, where you will dwell exactly seven years and three months.' To him likewise the shah replied: 'That is possible,' and he too disappeared, amid the jeers of the mob.

The competition lasted throughout the whole of that day and the next, to the delight of the people, until at last they thought of getting a certain Nasreddin, a wit well known throughout the East, to oppose to the shah.

On the third, and last, day appeared Nasreddin, tattered and almost naked, dragging with him two great clay jars. Addressing the shah, he said: 'Hail to the commander of the faithful, blessed be you name! You shall reign for another hundred years, and the love and confidence of your subjects will increase yearly.' 'That is possible,' said the shah. 'That the confidence your subjects repose in you is unbounded is evident from a fact which I am about to relate; you will doubtless deign to listen.' 'That is possible.' 'Your late father (God rest his soul!) was very friendly with my late father (may the

Prophet give him a place in Paradise!)...' 'That is possible.'
'Listen to me, O Shah! When your father went forth to war
with the unbelievers, he was so poor that he could not raise
an army.' 'That is possible.' 'Not only is it possible but true,
for, owing to his want of money, he borrowed from my father
these two jars full of gold pieces, and promised on his royal
word that you, O Shah, would pay your father's debt to me.'
Shah Ali burst into laughter, and said: 'That is impossible!
Your father was a tatterdemalion like yourself, and never saw
two jars of gold even in his dreams. Take your three hundred
gold pieces, and the devil take you. You rascal, you have outwitted me.'

THE KING'S SON

A certain king had a son, and sent him out to be nursed by a smith's wife. This crafty woman put the king's child in a common cradle, and her own son in the gorgeous royal cradle. Some years afterwards, the king took the changeling to court, and brought his foster-brother with him. One fine day, the king set out for his favorite forest to hunt, and took his pretended son with him. When they arrived, the king asked: 'How do you like this place, my son? Is it not a magnificent wood?' The boy replied: 'O father, if we could only burn it all somehow, what a fine lot of charcoal we should have!'

Then the king sent for the other boy, and asked him the same question. 'There could not be a better forest, your Majesty!' 'But what would you do with it if it were yours?' 'Nothing, your Majesty. I would double the guards, so that it should not be injured.' Then the king saw how the smith's wife had tried to cheat him, and put her in prison.

TEETH AND NO-TEETH

Shah Ali desired to see the hungriest man in his kingdom, and find out how much of the daintiest food such a man could eat at a meal. So he let it be known that on a certain day he would dine with his courtiers in the open air, in front of the palace. At the appointed hour, tables were laid and dinner was served, in the presence of a vast crowd. After the first course, the shah mounted a stand, and said: 'My loyal subjects! You see what a splendid dinner I have. I should like to share it with those among you who are really hungry, and have not eaten for a long time, so tell me truly which is the hungriest of you all, and bid him come forward.'

Two men appeared from the crowd: an old man of fifty and a young man of twenty-seven. The former was grey-haired and feeble, the latter was fresh and of athletic build.

'How is it that you are hungry?' asked the shah of the old man. 'I am old, my children are dead, toil has worn me out, and I have eaten nothing for three days.' 'And you?' said the shah, turning to the young man. 'I could not find work, and as I am a hearty young man I am ashamed to beg, so I too have not eaten for three days.' The shah ordered them to be given food, on one plate, and in small portions. The hungry men eagerly ate, watching each other intently. Suddenly the old man and the young one both stopped and began to weep. 'Why do you weep?' asked the shah in astonishment. 'I have no teeth,' said the old man, 'and while I am mumbling my food this young man eats up everything.' 'And why are you weeping?' 'He is telling lies, your majesty; while I am chewing my meat the old man gulps down everything whole...'

THE QUEEN'S WHIM

A certain queen wished to have a palace built of the bones of all kinds of birds. The king ordered birds to be caught, and the construction began. Bones of all kinds were brought and cleaned, and the walls were rising, but they could not find a hedge-sparrow, and, as the queen wanted all sorts of birds, a search was made for the missing one. At last the hedge-sparrow was found, and brought before the king, who asked where she had been. 'Mighty monarch! I have been flying all over the kingdom counting the men and women; unfortunately there are twice as many women as men.' The king ordered the bird to be punished for telling him such a shameless falsehood. 'King of kings,' said the hedge-sparrow, 'perhaps I did not count in the same way as you do.' 'How did you count, then?' 'I counted all those men who are under the slipper of women as old women.' The hedge-sparrow thus hinted that the king himself was an old woman, because he had not strength of mind enough to resist the foolish whims of his wife.

THE FOOL'S GOOD FORTUNE

A certain man died and left three sons. One was altogether a fool, another was fairly intelligent, and the third was rather clever. This being so, it was of course difficult for them to live together. In dividing the inheritance among them, the fool was cheated, and in regard to the cattle he was thus cozened: There were three entrances to the penfold, two open and one very narrow. The two clever brothers proposed to drive the beasts out of all three at once; those that issued from the small gap were to belong to the fool. In this way the latter's share was only one young bull out of the whole flock. But to his feeble mind the division seemed fair enough, so he contentedly drove his bull out into the forest, and tied it with a thick rope to a young tree, while he himself wandered aimlessly about.

Three days later, the fool went to see his beast. It had eaten and drunk nothing, but had pulled the tree up by the roots, and laid bare a jar full of old gold coins. The fool was delighted, and played with the money for a time, then he resolved to take the jar and present it to the king. As he passed along the road, every wayfarer looked into the pot, took out the gold in handfuls, and so that he should not notice their thefts, filled it up with stones and blocks of wood. On reaching the palace, the fool asked for an audience of the king, and it was granted. He emptied out the contents of the jar at the feet of the king. When the courtiers saw the wrath of the king, they took the fool away and beat him. When he had recovered himself he asked why he had been beaten. One of the bystanders, for fun, cried to him: 'You have been beaten because you labor in vain.' The fool went his way, muttering the words: 'You labor in vain.' As he passed a peasant who was reaping, he repeated his phrase again and again, until the peasant grew angry, and beat him. The fool asked why he had been beaten, and what he ought to have said. 'You ought to have said: "God give you a good harvest!"' The fool went on saying, 'God give you a good harvest!' and met a funeral. Again he was beaten, and again he asked what he should say. They replied that he should have said: 'Heaven rest your soul!' He then came to a wedding, and saluted the newly married couple with this funereal phrase. Again he was beaten, and then told that he should say: 'Be fruitful and multiply!' His next visit was to a monastery, and he accosted every monk with his new salutation. They too gave him a thrashing, with such vigor that the fool determined to have his revenge by stealing one of the bells from their belfry. So he hid himself until the monks had gone to rest, and then carried off a bell of moderate size. He went into the forest, climbed a tree, and hung the bell on the branches, ringing it from time to time, partly to amuse himself and partly to frighten away wild beasts. In the forest there was a gang of robbers, who were assembled to share their booty, and had just ended a merry banquet. Suddenly they heard the sound of the bell, and were much afraid. They took counsel as to what was to be done, and most of them were for flight, but the oldest of the band advised them to send a scout to see what was wrong. The bravest among them was sent to get information, and the rest remained as quiet as possible. The brigand went on tiptoe through the bushes to the tree where the fool was, and respectfully asked: 'Who are you? If you are an angel sent by God to punish our wickedness, pray spare us and we shall repent; if you are a devil from hell, come and share with us.' The fool was not so stupid that he did not see he had to deal with robbers, so he took out a knife, tolled the bell, and then said with a grave air: 'If you wish to know who I am, climb the tree and show me your tongue, so that I may mark on it who I am and what I ask of you.' The robber obediently climbed the tree, and put out his tongue as far as he could. The fool cut off his tongue, and kicked him to the ground. The robber, mad with pain, and frightened by his sudden fall, ran off howling. His comrades had come out to meet him, and when they saw the plight he was in they ran off in terror, leaving their wealth. Next morning the fool found the booty, and without saying anything to anybody, took it home and became much richer than his brothers. The fool built three palaces: one for himself, one for me, and one for you. There is merrymaking in the fool's palace—come and be one of the guests!

TWO LOSSES

During a great storm at sea, a learned man heard the skipper giving his orders, but could not understand a word. When the danger was past, he asked the skipper in what language he had spoken. The sailor replied: 'In my mother tongue, of course!' The scholar expressed his regret that a man should have wasted half his life without learning to speak grammatically and intelligibly. A few hours later the storm arose again, and this time the ship sprang a leak and began to founder. Then the captain went to the scholar and asked if he could swim. The man of books replied that he had never learned. 'I am sorry, sir, for you will lose your whole life. The ship will go to the bottom in a minute, and my crew and I shall swim ashore. You would have done well if you had spent a little of your time in learning to swim.'

THE STORY OF DERVISH

A hunter killed a stag in the mountains, and began to skin it. He then hung the skin on a bush, and went down to a stream to wash the blood from his hands. When he came back, he found to his surprise that the dead stag had come to life, and was running away. When he had recovered from his astonishment, he chased the beast, but could not overtake it, and it was soon lost to sight. He met a wayfarer, briefly told him the story, and asked if he had ever seen a stag without a skin. 'I have never seen a stag without skin, but I do not wonder at your story. Near here there is a healing spring where any beast, even if wounded unto death, can be cured by bathing. Your stag probably bathed there, and is now sound and well. But if you want to know more about this wonderful country of ours, seek out a man called Dervish, and he will tell you things that will soon make you forget all about the stag.' 'Where can I find this Dervish?' asked the hunter. 'Go from village to village, and look into every courtyard, and when you see a man smoking a pipe, with an ass and a she-ass bound before him, ask him.'

The hunter went away, and, after a long search, found Dervish, who told him the following story:

'I was married,' said Dervish, 'and loved my wife, but she deceived me with my next-door neighbor. When I heard of this I questioned my wife, but, instead of answering, she struck me with a whip, and, to my horror, I was turned into a dog. My wife drove me out into the yard, and for shame I ran away. On the road I suffered hunger, thirst, and despair, and, for the first time in my life, I knew what it was to be powerless, and realized what a great difference there is between man and beast. When I opened my mouth and tried to speak, I only barked and howled. I tried to stand on my hind legs, and walk like a man, but I fell either backwards or forwards. Then I jumped about, and did this so easily and briskly that I regained my spirits, and came to think that even a dog's life had its pleasures. While I was merrily jumping, I unexpectedly saw a man. He looked at me and I at him. The man smiled, and I ran up to him, but he was afraid, and lifted his stick to strike me. We both moved away from each other. I wanted to speak, but I barked, and the man raised his stick again. I then began to frolic and jump, and the man smiled again, and let me come up to him. I understood how dog and man are always the best of friends, and in my mind I thanked my wicked wife that she had turned me into a dog, and not some other beast, a pig, for instance. The man who beckoned me to come to him was a good village priest, and we soon became great friends. He caressed me, gave me something to eat, and I went away with him. The kind-hearted priest, overcome by the heat, lay down to rest under a tree, and I wished to do the same, but the priest said: "Watch over me!" so I did not go to sleep, rightly thinking that if the priest woke and found me asleep he would give me no more bread, and perhaps would drive me away. Ah! The beginning of my dog life was grievous. In the evening, the priest stopped to sleep with some shepherds who were watching their flocks. The shepherds, to show honor to their pastor, killed a lamb for supper, got wine, and made merry. Though I took no direct part in the feast, I kept close behind my master. After supper, one of the shepherds looked at me, and said: "This dog must be fond of wine, for he never takes his eyes from the glass, and now and then he licks his lips." I nodded my head several times. Then the shepherds poured me out some wine in a plate, and I lapped it up with plea-sure. When they were all asleep, wolves came and attacked the sheep. The shepherds' dogs barked, but did not dare to attack the wolves; I rose and killed three wolves on the spot. When the shepherds saw this, they offered the priest a good price for me, and he finally sold me. Before long I had killed a vast number of wolves, and the fame of me reached the ears of the king of the country. I was brought and taken to the palace, to the sick daughter of the king, who was tormented at night by brownies. Every morning the princess woke exhausted and feeble. On the first night of my watch, I saw swans enter the bedchamber through the closed doors; they choked and tram-pled upon the sleeping princess. I was chained up, and could do nothing to help the poor maiden. In the morning, I was scolded for not having done anything, but one of the courtiers defended me, saying: "He is a good dog, but he must be un-chained, and then we shall see what he can do." Next night the swans came again. I killed ten of them, but the eleventh asked me to spare her, saying she would help me in the matter of my wife and our neighbor. I trusted the swan, and let her go. To my delight, the princess rose healyou and merry next morn-ing. The king was exceedingly pleased with me, and ordered me to have a heavy gold chain, and to be fed right royally. I lived well in the palace, but I longed to see my home and wife again, so I soon ran away. When I entered my own house, my wife took off my gold chain, struck me with her whip, and turned me into a duck. I flew into a field near by, where millet had been sown, and, being inexperienced, was caught at once in nets laid by a peasant. The peasant took me under his arm, and gave me to his wife, telling her to cook me for dinner. As soon as the peasant had gone out, the woman looked at me intently, and then took down from the wall a whip, with which she struck me, and turned me into a man again, saying: "Have I helped you or not? We were twelve sisters, you killed ten of us, I am the eleventh, and your wife is the twelfth. Now go home, take the whip which hangs over your wife's bed, strike her and your neighbor with it, and you can turn them into any kind of beasts that you wish." I went in late at night, when my wife and the neighbor were both asleep, I struck them with the whip, and turned my wife into an ass, and the man into a she-ass, and here they are.' The hunter was terrified when he heard this story of Dervish, he ran away from the enchanted mountain realm as fast as he could, and resolved never to go back there again.

THE FATHER'S PROPHESY

A certain man often told his son, while beating him, that he would never come to any good. The boy grew tired of these rebukes, and ran away from home. Ten years later he had risen to the rank of Pasha[31], and was set over the very Pashalik[32] where his father lived. On his way to his post, the new Pasha stopped at a place twenty miles off, and said to the Bashi-Bazouks[33] of his guard: 'Ride to such and such a village, seize so and so, and bring him to me.' The Bashi-Bazouks arrived at night, dragged the sick old man out of bed, and took him to the Pasha. The Pasha stretched himself to his full height, and, ordering the old man to look him in the face, said: 'Do you know me?' The old man fixed his gaze on the pasha, and cried: 'Ah, Pasha! You are surely my son.' 'Did you not tell me in my boyhood that I should never come to any good? Now look at me,' and the Pasha pointed to his epaulets. 'Well, was I wrong? You are no man, but only a Pasha. What man would send for his father in the way you have done? I repeat it, you have gained the rank of Pasha, but you have not become a good man.'

---

31 A Pasha is a high-ranking Turkish officer.
32 A Pashalik is the jurisdiction of a Pasha.
33 Bashi-bazouks were the irregular guards of the Turkish army.

THE HERMIT PHILOSOPHER

There was once a wise man who loved solitude, and dwelt far away from other men, meditating on the vanities of the world. He spent nearly all his time in the open air, and he could easily do this, for he lived in a lovely southern land where there is no winter and but little rain. As he wandered once among the verdure of his garden, the sage stopped before an aged walnut tree covered with ripening nuts, and said: 'Why is there such a strange want of symmetry in nature? Here, for instance, is a walnut tree a hundred years old, hiding its top in the clouds, and yet how small is its fruit: itself it grows from year to year, but its fruit is always of the same size. Now, on the beds at the foot of the tree there grow great pumpkins and melons on very small creeping plants. It would be more fitting if the pumpkins grew on the walnut trees and the walnuts on the pumpkin beds. Why this want of symmetry in nature?' The sage thought deeply on the subject, and walked in the garden for a long time, till at last he felt sleepy. He layed down under the shady walnut tree, and was soon sleeping peacefully. In a short time, he felt a slight blow on the face, then a second, and then a third. As he opened his eyes, a ripe walnut fell on his nose. The sage leaped to his feet, and said: 'Now I understand the secret of nature. If this tree had borne melons or pumpkins, my head would have been broken. Henceforth let no one presume to find fault with Providence!'

THE KING'S COUNSELLOR

The counsellor of an Arabian king once thought to himself that, though he had lived so many years, and knew so much, he had never yet found out how much the king valued his services, and to what extent his wife and friends really loved him. He decided to try them all at once, so he went to the palace and stole a goat of which the king was very fond, and of which he was the keeper. He then went home, told this secret to his wife, and in her presence ordered the cook to roast the goat. But afterwards he privately told the cook to hide the royal goat, and roast a kid in its place. At supper his wife praised the dish very highly. As soon as the king heard of the loss of his goat, he was very angry, and cried in his wrath: 'If any man finds the thief I shall load him with gold, if a woman finds him I shall marry her!' The counselor's wife, thinking it better to be a king's wife, betrayed her husband. The king ordered his counsellor to be executed, and married the woman. When the execution was about to take place, the victim's old friends succeeded in saving him by a large bribe, and another criminal was executed instead. The counsellor was hidden in a neighboring realm. Some years afterwards, troublesome questions of state arose, and none of the council could solve them. The king often longed for his old counsellor, and said: 'For the sake of a goat I sacrificed a clever man, if he were alive he would get me out of all my trouble in a day.' The counsellor's old friends at last resolved to acknowledge the trick they had played. So one day, when the king was in a good humor, they went and said: 'Pardon us, O king! Your first counsellor is alive!' and they told him all. The king was heartily glad, and ordered the exile to be brought back. He was well received, and restored the goat to the king. The king said: 'My friend! We thus see that the greatest scourge of all is false witness, and that we must beware, above all things, of our wives.'

A WITTY ANSWER

A certain king was angry with one of his lords, and put him in prison; wishing to keep him there, he said he would only set him free if he could bring to the court a horse which was neither grey, black, brown, white, chestnut, nor piebald—and, in short, the king enumerated every possible color that a horse could be. The imprisoned lord promised to get such a horse if the king would set him free at once. As soon as he was at liberty, the lord asked the king to send a groom for the horse, but begged that the groom might come neither on Monday nor Tuesday, Wednesday nor Thursday, Friday, Saturday, nor Sunday, but on any other day of the week that suited His Majesty.

THE WAGTAIL BIRD

The little wagtail bird is so stupid, that when the thunder be-
gins to roll it lies down on its back, and thinks: "If the sky
falls, I shall hold it up with my foot, so that the world will not
be crushed."